AFTER THE BOMB

Gloria Miklowitz

SCHOLASTIC INC.
New York Toronto London Auckland Sydney Tokyo

In a dark time, the eye begins to see.
—THEODORE ROETHKE

ISBN 0-590-33287-2

12 11 10 9 8 7 6 5 4 3 2 1   1   5 6 7 8 9/8 0/9

Printed in the U.S.A.   01

AFTER THE BOMB

NOTE

The events in this book, while fictitious, are based on what might well happen in the event of a single, one-megaton bomb falling on any large city in the world.

The author's assumptions as to the degree and extent of damage and the level of assistance likely to come to survivors are based on extensive reading and interviews.

Books read include: *The Final Epidemic*, Physicians and Scientists on Nuclear War, edited by Ruth Adams and Susan Cullen; *Fate of the Earth*, by Jonathan Schell; *Hiroshima*, by John Hershey; *Hiroshima No Pika*, by Toshi Maruki. Other readings were from numerous newspaper and magazine articles.

Those interviewed include: Dr. Aron Kupperman, California Institute of Technology; Ernest Benson, Engineer, Dept. of Water and Power, Pasadena, Ca.; Jean Ehret, emergency room nurse, Verdugo Hill Hospital, Montrose, Ca.; Michael Regan, head of Civil Defense for the City of Los Angeles; Capt. King, La Canada Fire Department; Nurse Julie McGoldrick, Sherman Oaks Burn Center; Staff Sgt. Moore, U. S. Marine Corps Disaster Control in Santa Ana; Maj. Llarena, National Guard, Arcadia, Ca.; and Col. Andrew Wolf, National Guard, Sacramento, Ca..

Chapter 1

Eyes closed, Philip yawned, stretched his arms wide, and wished he could have stayed in bed another hour. Behind him the radio droned pleasantly and the blender whirred his breakfast shake of milk, eggs, wheat germ, honey, and juice.

". . . six twenty-eight on this bright, beautiful morning, folks. Weatherman predicts a high in the eighties and a low around fifty. For those on the freeways, watch out for flying debris. Reports of an overturned vehicle. . . ."

Philip peered groggily out the kitchen window, both hands resting on the sink. A brown film dusted the hills across the valley. He scratched his leg just below his maroon running shorts and noted how the wind tugged the Catalina cherry bushes along the driveway and how gusts bent the pine tree in the Giaimo's yard, next door.

Horgan said they'd have to do ten miles today, up and down those hills across the way. "Good for stamina," he'd said, hard eyes challenging them to complain. "Thursday you're gonna beat San Marino. Right?"

"Right," the team had echoed in unison.

At least he wouldn't sweat. It was a dry, hot wind coming from the desert, pushing the smog out to sea. It'd be easy running those first five miles. The wind would push him. But coming back was something else. It would be like pulling weights, and that dust would make it hard to breathe, not to mention how it made him itch and gave him nosebleeds.

He switched off the blender, removed the lid, and lifted the pitcher to his lips. Holding it in both hands, he tilted his head back the way his brother Matt always did, and drank.

". . . in world news today, TASS, the official Soviet news agency, announced that the recent American nuclear buildup will force the Soviet Union to —"

With one hand he switched the dial.

". . . terrorists say that if their demands are not met by noon tomorrow, the hostages —"

He made a sour face and switched the dial again. News could be so boring. Nothing but this guy killing that one. More taxes, more money going to defense. *Boring*. What could he do about any of it, anyway? If you thought too much about all the rotten things that could happen in the world you'd go nuts. Besides, there were enough things he

2

couldn't do anything about right here, at home and at school.

He found a station he liked better, and the soothing voice of a young woman came on. He put the blender bowl in the sink, wondering what she looked like. "K-I-I-S," she sang in that sultry, warm voice he liked so much in Cara. "Los An-ge-lus."

"Nuts!" he exclaimed, hearing the quick, angry blast of Tim's car horn. He'd asked his friend not to do that. It woke his parents and made them mad. "You should be out there waiting so he wouldn't have to wake up the whole neighborhood," his mom had said. Yeah. Now it was too late. Even too late to go to the john.

Taking the steps two at a time, he chased back to his bedroom and rummaged under the stack of unhung clothes on the chair for his day pack. His jeans turned up at the foot of the bed, and the Government text was on the floor next to the frayed notebook with Cara's name all over it. "You live like a pig," Matt was always saying. Phil always answered, "You're compulsively neat. I bet you had severe toilet training." It was a running argument.

The horn blasted again, longer, more insistently.

"Damn," he whispered. He stuffed his books into the pack, checked twice for lunch money, and bolted from the room.

"Phil!"

"Yeah, *what*?" He popped his head around

the door to his brother's room. "What? I'm late!"

Sitting up in bed on one elbow, Matt glared at him. "Can't you keep it down?"

"Turkey!"

"Nerd!" he heard yelled after him.

"Same to you," he mumbled as he raced down the stairs.

"We're gonna be late," Tim announced as Philip climbed in the car. "Horgan's gonna have our tails." He took off down the driveway with a squeal of rubber.

"Couldn't get up. Studied till after two for that dumb math test, and I still don't feel prepared."

"You never feel prepared. Then you always get a hundred. How's the knee?"

He shrugged. It hurt but somehow he could handle the pain. "I'm supposed to go easy on it for a few days but fat chance with Horgan after me." He turned to look at his friend. "Going to the dance tonight?"

"I don't know."

"Matt's going. With Cara."

"Figures."

It still hurt that Matt had taken Cara away just when he'd been ready to ask her out. After all, he'd seen her first, been the first to talk when she moved in down the block.

"She's beautiful," he'd told Matt.

"With those railroad tracks? Your taste is in your toes."

And when he'd included Cara in their hikes, Matt would ask, "Why'd you invite that airhead along?"

But that was last year. Now you couldn't pry Matt from Cara with a crowbar. And he couldn't blame Cara. Who'd want *him*? Sixteen going on twelve, the way he looked. Who'd go for a skinny bean of a guy whose chin hairs could be counted on one hand and whose shoulders and butt measured the same?

"So?" Tim repeated, pulling into the high school parking lot just next to the gym. "You going?"

Horgan's Heroes, as the track team was called, were goose-stepping out of the gym in their warm-up exercises. Philip pulled his day pack from the car and slammed the door. "I hate going alone. I get all nervous and sweaty and say such dumb things."

Tim fell in beside him. "At least you talk. Me? I go blank."

"So let's go together. We'll have each other to talk to." Philip stiffened as Horgan came out of the gym.

"Hey, you guys!" the coach shouted. "Get the lead out of your butts! Outside warming up in one minute or you can add two miles to the ten!"

Philip broke into a run. When he reached his locker, his fingers fumbled, and it took him two tries to open the lock. He always got so nervous when Horgan got mad like that, when anyone got angry with him, in fact.

If it had been Matt, he'd have given Horgan one of those cool, measured looks with those piercing eyes of his. And then he'd have strolled on to his locker as if he had all day.

"When are you picking up Cara?" Philip asked later. He was standing in front of the mirror in Matt's room, peering at his image, wondering if he should shave the few hairs on his chin or leave them alone. Didn't hair grow faster if you cut it often?

"Right after dinner." Matt lifted the player arm on his turntable and ever so cautiously set the needle down. The opening notes of Beethoven's Fifth Symphony filled the room. He turned up the volume.

Sometimes Philip wondered if Matt really needed to hear the music that loud or if he liked everyone to know that he listened to classical music. He picked up his guitar and slumped against the bed on the floor. Strumming chords, he tuned out the noise.

"Get out of here if you're going to play that now!" Matt turned on him abruptly. "Go on, out!"

"The trouble with you, brother, is you can't concentrate on more than one thing at a time. Weak brain." Philip tapped his head with a finger and grinned. The only time Matt noticed him was when he did something irritating. "Mom's calling. You deaf?"

Matt turned down the volume, frowning.

"Matt? Do you hear me?" their mother

called. "Come on down. I need you to slice the roast. Matt?"

"Why doesn't she ever need *you*?" Matt exclaimed. He stuck his head out of the door to tell her he'd be right there. Then he took his time removing the record, sliding it into its jacket and placing it back on the shelf exactly where he always kept it. Philip, watching, continued to strum his guitar. Why *hadn't* Mom called him to carve the roast? he wondered. She hardly ever asked him to do any of the more interesting things. He put down the guitar and decided to see what was going on downstairs.

Mom greeted them with a smile. Philip guessed she was behind with the laundry again because she wore Matt's T-shirt, which on her was two sizes too big; a paint-spattered pair of jeans; and sneakers. The shirt said: "One Nuclear Bomb Can Ruin Your Entire Day."

"Sharpen the carving knife first, Matt." She nodded at the roast and bent to find the carving board. "And slice it thin."

"I can do it!" Philip darted around his brother and grabbed for the knife, but Matt stopped his hand.

"Down, boy. You'd probably slice off a finger."

"Mom!"

His mother hesitated, then said, "You set the table for us, honey. Dad's due home any minute."

"I'm just as good at carving as he is!"

"Philip, please."

"Setting the table is girl's work!"

"Philip!"

He yanked at the silverware drawer, and everything fell to the floor.

Matt stifled a laugh.

His mother sighed, gave him an annoyed scowl, and bent to help pick up the pieces.

Hating himself for such clumsiness, he tried a joke. "Teenage boys grow so fast, they're not very well coordinated."

Matt snorted and whisked the knife back and forth over the sharpening tool, eyes on Philip.

"Well, it's true! Okay, so I made it up, but it's probably true." When his mother looked doubtful, he added, "Any time you need a useful fact, just ask me. I make them up to suit any occasion."

His mother shook her head and giggled. Matt's face broke into a reluctant grin. It would be all right.

"So, how's my family?" his father asked at dinner, helping himself to a slice of beef. He nodded to each of them. "How's school?"

"Hard," his mother answered first. "I have two papers to finish by next week and an exam to study for. This roast is going to be the last good meal you have for a while. After this, it's leftovers."

"What about you, Matt? Get that chemistry test grade yet?"

"I did okay, I guess. B minus."

Philip darted a glance at his brother. Matt had been so nervous the night before the test that he'd thrown up. He was funny that way. No matter how confidently he talked or acted, his stomach always gave him away. But no one outside of the family knew that.

"And you, Phil? How'd the math test go?" his father asked.

He'd gotten a ninety-seven but wasn't about to boast about it, especially now, after Matt's news, so he said, "Pretty good. And how was your tiddlywink game today, Dad?"

It was a family joke dating back to when they were kids, that all their father did at work was play tiddlywinks. What he really did, Philip now understood, was sit at a desk all day solving humongous equations, which made any math Philip knew look like child's play. Somehow the solutions helped engineers build things, like bomb silos.

"You know," his mother mused before his father could answer, "we talked about the mess the world's in in poli. sci. class today. I said that if women were running the world there'd be no wars. I think I'm going to run for public office when I get my degree."

"Ha," Matt said. "Last week you were ready to run off to Africa to study pygmies."

"And the week before you were going to be a social worker," his father said.

"Mom? What *are* you going to be when you grow up?" Philip ducked as his mother took a playful swipe at him.

"It's not funny, you guys. We've got forty-seven wars going on in the world today, and you're making jokes. And the way the U.S. and Russia are talking. . . ."

"Ma? When're you going to do another wash? I'm out of socks. I'm out of everything," Matt said.

"I've got socks," Philip said.

"You? Not on your life! Yours are so grungy, I'm surprised they don't get up and walk away."

"Boy. Try to start an intelligent conversation around here!" His mother shook her head then turned to Matt. "Honey chile, if you need clean clothes so badly, you know what you do? You go into the laundry room, and there's this rectangular white object. It's called a washing machine. And you take —"

"Okay, okay. I get it." Matt rolled his eyes skyward.

"You look pretty sharp to me," Philip said, looking his brother over. Matt's dark good looks and manly build made anything he wore look good.

"Yeah?"

"Sure. The girls'll be all over you. You'll have to cut them away with a blowtorch. And Cara —"

"*Philip!*" his mother warned.

He reacted by sitting up very properly, hands clasped. "Yes, ma'am."

"Let's clear the dishes. You guys have a

dance to go to, and you're not going to leave me with all the work. Up."

Philip jumped to his feet. "First a *hoo*." He pounced on his mother as she started out of the room, dishes in hand.

"Philip, no!"

"Just one." He grabbed her from behind and squeezed so that her breath came out in a *whoosh*, making a *hoo* sound. He squeezed again.

"Philip, leave me alone!"

Every time Philip *hoo*ed his mother, she laughed, so he did it again. But she wasn't laughing now. She turned around and cried, "Stop it! Don't be a pest! Enough's enough!"

"Okay, okay." He retreated, picked up some dishes, and went into the kitchen, hurt. A look passed between Matt and his parents that he didn't like, as if they were all in on something together, excluding him.

When was this family going to treat him like he counted, like they treated Matt?

Chapter 2

Philip unscrewed the bottle of aftershave lotion that belonged to Matt and sniffed. It had a fresh smell, like limes. He splashed some in his hand and patted it against his cheek and on his neck the way Matt did. He was conscious of his brother behind him. Matt was neatly folding a sweater and watching.

"You making it with Cara yet?" He turned around to face Matt.

"If you're going to use my stuff, put the cap back on the bottle when you're through and put it away."

He screwed the cap on and put the bottle down. "You making it with Cara yet?"

Matt's dark eyes burned into him for a long instant, then he said, "How are you getting to the dance?"

"Tim."

"I'll give you a ride if you want. Cara won't mind."

"No, thanks." He tugged angrily at the

Mexican shirt that wouldn't stay on his narrow shoulders and hung too loosely over his jeans. Maybe he should wear something else.

"Why don't you wear that blue plaid shirt of yours?" Matt, said, reading his thoughts. "You look much better in it." He picked up his wallet and keys. "Your guitar's gonna get stepped on."

"Yes, Mommy. I pick up my guitar, Mommy."

Matt shook his head in disgust. "See you at the dance, Phil." He took one last look around to see if everything was in order and left.

Philip picked up his guitar and plopped down on Matt's neatly made bed, shoes on. He got a perverse pleasure out of doing what might make his brother angry. Plucking at the strings, he reworked a song written last week and thought about Cara. Did she ever think about *him*? Where would she and Matt go after the dance? To the Straw Hat with friends? Or would they drive up into the hills and make out? For a few pleasurable moments he pictured himself with Cara, just holding her hand. Maybe kissing her like he almost did once.

And then he went into his own room to take off the ugly Mexican shirt and put on the blue plaid.

Tim arrived soon after, wearing dark pants, a short-sleeved white shirt, and shiny black shoes. He tugged at the tie.

"You look good," Philip said.

"You, too. Nice shirt."

His friend's compliment helped ease the big knot in his stomach. Tonight he intended to have a really good time. No matter how scared he felt, he'd ask some girls to dance instead of just standing around as he usually did, watching. Maybe he'd even ask Cara.

When they got to the school gym, the dance was in full swing. They could hear the music outside, where so many of the kids hung around. Philip searched around anxiously for someone he knew.

"There's Cara!" His heart leaped as he saw her beside Matt. Soft blonde hair swirled around her face. She wore a pink dress with little purple flowers and she held it close to her leg with one hand, against the wind.

"Wow," Tim murmured. "The girls sure go for your brother. Just look at them."

Four girls clustered around Matt like birds at a feeder. It happened all the time at school. Girls would go stiff and watchful, and when he passed, they'd huddle together and whisper.

"Let's go," Philip said to Tim. "I have nothing against Matt's leftovers."

Tim chuckled, and they sauntered across the quad to Matt and Cara's side.

"Hi, Phil," Cara greeted with a warm smile. "Hi, Tim. You guys know each other? Joyce, Courtney, Liz, Pat. This is Philip, Matt's brother, and Tim, his friend."

Philip smiled brightly. The girls checked

him and Tim over quickly and returned their attention to Matt.

"You mean it's a real air-raid shelter, like they show in war movies?" the girl who'd been introduced as Courtney exclaimed. "Like underground and all? And it's all your very own?"

"Matt and Phil use it as a clubhouse, sort of," Cara said. "A getaway. We play games down there sometimes and pretend we're the only people left in the world, or sometimes we make believe we're on a desert island and —"

"But who built it, for heaven's sake? And why?" Pat asked.

"Don't know. It was there when we bought the house. My dad fixed it up. You know, new generator and bunk beds and stuff. They said there was a war scare years ago when the Russians put up bases in Cuba," Matt said.

"Can I see it? Oh, can I? I've never been in an air-raid shelter. It sounds *neat*!" Courtney looked eagerly at Matt. Philip grinned at Tim and raised his eyebrows.

Philip cleared his throat. "*I'll* be glad to take you down there. Just say when."

Courtney's glance slid over him. "Matt? Will you show me? If there's ever a war can I go into it with you?"

The girls giggled. Matt rolled his eyes skyward and said, "Let's go, Cara." But he didn't move.

Boring, Philip thought. How could Cara

stand it? Still, they were female. He looked the four girls over and discounted Pat and Courtney immediately. They were so eager for Matt, they looked like they could eat him. Liz, who hadn't said a word, wore a dazed smile. Maybe Joyce. She wasn't bad. She was about his height, freckled, maybe a bit plump — but pretty. And a little aloof. He sidled closer to her. While the others fired questions at Matt, he nudged her. She didn't notice at first, so he nudged a little harder.

"*What?*" she asked irritably.

"Wanna go inside and dance?" Heat rushed to his head.

"No."

He took a deep breath and looked away, pretending to be interested in some distant spot. Was he that ugly? That unpleasant? He wanted to sniff under his arms and blow into his hand to see if he smelled okay. Why had he ever come?

"Phil?"

His throat constricted. He was afraid to talk for fear it would come out funny.

"Want to dance? We'll never be missed." Cara took his arm. "Tim? Come on. I'll introduce you to someone I think you'll like. We'll be inside, Matt," she called back. Matt nodded and went on talking.

"He can't help it," Cara said, walking between them and linking her arms with theirs. "He really doesn't like all that attention, but sometimes they corral him. He's just being polite, but he really hates it. Really."

"Yeah, sure," Philip said.

"I wouldn't mind a night of that kind of hateful attention," Tim said.

"You guys just wait. By next year you'll be complaining that girls are phoning you all the time. Now, just listen to that music. Doesn't it make you want to go? Come on! Let's dance!"

Philip figured he had maybe two minutes before Matt came looking for them. Longer, if he could manage it. He pulled Cara through the mass of jumping, bouncing, gesticulating dancers in the crowded, noisy gym. He was counting on another few minutes if they could hide where the flickering lights made it even harder to see anyone.

Sweating, heart pounding, he turned to face Cara, worried she might laugh at his clumsiness. The throbbing music pounded at his head, ran up through his feet. Cara's eyes danced. She was the most beautiful girl on the floor. He'd always pictured dancing with her like this. He flung his arms around and felt as if he really knew what he was doing. Cara had always put him at ease.

"Remember the Halloween party we planned last year?" he shouted above the deafening noise. They'd spent happy hours together working out the party details. His smiled faded. It was also the night Matt first really noticed Cara.

"Yeah!" she cried. "Grapes for eyeballs. Cooked spaghetti for innards." She laughed. "What kid stuff! But wasn't it fun?"

He nodded. "What's Matt got that I haven't?" he shouted, willing her to look at him.

"Oh, Phil. . . ."

"Well?" In the intense excitement he bumped into a girl dancing behind him.

"You have lots of qualities."

"Name one."

"Persistence."

"Oh, yeah. A lot of good that does. All it does is make people mad at me."

"It's a fine quality!"

Discounting her words, he shrugged. "What else?"

"You're fun."

"So's Matt."

"Not always." Her eyes slid away for an instant.

"What else?"

"Greedy, aren't you?" She laughed. Shaking her body so her dress swung around her legs, she said, "You're great at math. You're a terrific runner."

"Who says?"

"Matt."

The answer came as such a surprise that he stumbled against her. *Matt said nice things about him to Cara?* He didn't tell her what a slob he was, how clumsy, what a pest? God, he loved that brother of his at this moment. He admired, worshiped, even envied him!

Cara cocked her head in a teasing way.

The music had stopped, but he went on dancing until she put a hand on his arm. "Surprised?"

"Shocked."

"Freeze, pardner!" A voice from behind him sounded like Matt. Something jabbed him in the back. "Okay, move away slowly or I'll plug ya."

Cara laughed.

Unhand my woman, and run for your life."

"Turkey!" Philip turned around and playfully punched his brother in the gut.

"What's this you're shocked about?" Matt asked, arm around Cara.

"At the number of females you manage to fool."

"*Charm*, not fool."

"So? Did you line up those girls to come see your secret lair?" Cara asked.

Matt hugged her closer. "I told them to show up Saturday afternoon. That's when we give the half-rate tour. I told them to bring refreshments, and if they're lucky, my little brother would play his guitar, so they'd get a show along with the tour."

"*Little brother*? You didn't! You're kidding!" Philip's heart jumped with hope.

Matt smiled. "Am I?"

"Well, if they come, it will be only because of you."

Matt had already lost interest in the subject and turned back to Cara. At the same time the P.A. system crackled and then burst forth with the next dance number. His brother and Cara started dancing.

For an instant Philip remained where he was. Dancers bounced against him, jammed into him. Then, sighing happily, he turned around and worked his way through the crowd looking for Tim.

Chapter 3

When he came down to breakfast Monday morning at a normal time, everyone except Matt was still eating.

"Not running today?" His father looked up from the paper.

"After school. Horgan's hoping the wind will die down so it won't be so dusty."

"Just look out there!" His mother leaned on the sink and peered out of the window with worried concern. "I'm afraid even to leave the house. The hills haven't burned around here in years. With this wind, a little fire would spread like. . . ." She threw up her hands. "You did increase our fire insurance, didn't you, Allen?"

His father nodded.

Philip poured himself some juice and brought it to the table. He reached for the sports section of the paper.

"No health-food cocktail today?"

"Today I feel like junk food. Some nice

sugar-coated crispies, and the heck with Horgan. So I die a day sooner."

"Talk about dying," his father said, "did you see this piece in the paper about the new missile deployment system? As if there aren't enough nuclear bombs already! Nice world we're living in."

Philip tuned out as his parents began discussing the news story. Something about fifty thousand nuclear bombs in storage, between Russia and the U.S. That was a lot. If he ran ten miles a day every day for a year, how long would it take to make fifty thousand miles? He calculated the problem roughly in his head. *Fourteen years. Five thousand one hundred and ten days.* Phew!

"Philip! Doesn't anything interest you other than sports?"

"Sure. Music. Girls." He took a big mouthful of cereal and grabbed for a paper napkin as milk spilled down his chin.

"You're hopeless."

"You grown-ups built the bomb. It's up to you to do something about it. Anyway, if anything happens we can always go live in the shelter."

His father looked appalled. "I can't believe you said that!" he exclaimed.

"Said what?"

"Finish your breakfast and get to school," his mother said. "We'll argue about this another time."

He hated it when his parents put him down that way. Usually he wasn't even sure what he'd said wrong. They made him feel like they had no respect for his opinions. Matt claimed it was because he jumped into discussions without facts, then stubbornly clung to his viewpoint when he knew he was wrong. But how else could he survive in a family where everyone, except him, was perfect?

The feeling of being at odds with the world continued through the morning. In English class he deliberately took an extreme viewpoint in interpreting a scene from *Hamlet*. In economics class he took the unpopular view about whether the world should go off the gold standard. It was one of those days when he couldn't seem to stop himself from doing the very opposite of what everyone else did.

Grumpy and hungry, he waited for Matt and Cara in the cafeteria at noon, reading the menu again and again. Should he get the spaghetti, macaroni and cheese, or a hamburger? If he chose the spaghetti he'd be sorry it hadn't been the burger. If he chose the burger, he'd wish later he'd bought the macaroni.

"Hey, little brother. Forgot my lunch money. Lend me a couple?"

Philip turned to Matt, his glance first gliding over Cara, and took out his wallet. "You still owe me for last week's lunch."

"Listen to him." Matt nodded to Cara. "A mind like a dollar sign. You'd think I was asking to borrow a million."

"I'll lend you the money, Matt," Cara said.

"No, here!" Phil hurriedly handed over two dollars. Instead of coming out the good guy, he was being made to look the villain. How come his brother always managed to come out looking right, even when he was wrong?

"Thanks, pal. Pay you back tonight." Matt tucked the money in his shirt pocket, flicked his eyes over the menu, and picked up a tray. He went directly to the macaroni and cheese. Philip decided to take the same, and followed his brother and Cara to a table.

"How's Maybelle?" Cara asked, unloading her tray. Dressed in an orange cheerleader skirt and blue-and-orange sweater, she looked happy and fresh.

He grinned sheepishly. Maybelle was a mystery lady the track team was always talking about. She was supposed to live on Vista del Valle. The guys said she had a thing for high school men, especially Horgan's Heroes. Sometimes, the stories went, if you were out running alone she'd be waiting, a glass of white wine in each hand.

"You know Jimmy? Well, he saw her just last week. He said she was wearing this flowing thing . . . a negligee." His whole body got hot, talking to Cara like that. "She waved at him and then —"

"Oh, sure," Matt said.

"Yeah, sure!" Philip returned. He really didn't quite believe it himself, but whenever he ran on Vista del Valle, he'd slow down, just in case.

"You must still believe in Santa Claus."

"There has to be something to it. Everyone says —"

"You believe everything you hear?"

"Oh, you're so smart. You never believe anything you hear!"

"Hey, you guys, quit that!" Cara put a hand on each of them. "For two brothers who really like each other, you sure try hard to hide it!"

Philip busied himself with spooning up the macaroni. What a turkey that brother of his was! He could be such a smart-ass. And he had the heart of a lizard. What right did he have to move in on Cara? "You got anything going with her?" Matt had asked last year. " 'Cause if you don't, I'm gonna ask her out."

He still got mad at himself for not speaking up. But what could he have said? There hadn't really been anything between him and Cara except what went on in his dreams. And even if he'd asked Cara, what chance did he stand with a brother like Matt?

"Gotta go, guys. Tennis practice." Matt gathered up his lunch things and stood up. "See you later, Cara. Usual place." He nodded curtly at Philip, then sauntered off, bookbag slung over one shoulder. The girls at the next table looked up and waved a greeting.

"Don't mind him so much," Cara said

softly. "Sometimes he does come on a little strong."

"My brother's a . . . turkey," Philip said.

"That he is. Sometimes. But aren't we all, sometimes?" Cara smiled that warm, impish smile that always made him melt inside. His body relaxed. Matt didn't deserve a girl like her.

He waved at his mother as he trudged up the driveway after school. She was staking a pine tree he'd helped his father plant last year. The tree leaned toward the Giaimos', house, its needles pushed by the wind.

"Need help?" he called.

"Almost done. Thanks, honey. Get yourself a snack, then come on out." His mother motioned to the lawn, covered with leaves, and blew him a kiss. He laughed and did a little happy dance, then went on into the house.

In a few minutes his mother appeared. Barefoot, in shorts and a halter top, she had the distracted look she wore much of the time since she had gone back to college. He really was proud of her, but he hardly ever saw her anymore because she was often in her room studying when he got home. He missed the way they used to talk, missed just having her around.

"Lemonade?" she asked, going to the refrigerator. "Horgan ought to be shot having you guys run on a day like this." Taking a glass from the cabinet, she poured the drink without waiting for his answer and set out some store-bought cookies.

"I'm not hungry." He tossed his books on the family room couch.

"How about I fix you a nice, thick, ham sandwich?" she asked, not really listening. "You're so skinny, it worries me. It really does." She glanced at her watch, trying not to be obvious. "I've got such a lot to do. That paper on abused children is due tomorrow, and I'm only half through. Haven't even thought what to make for dinner yet, and. . . ." She stopped, frowned, then asked, "How's school?"

"That's okay, Mom. Go finish your work. We'll talk later. What do you want me to do outside?"

"Oh, that, yes." She stopped for a moment and looked at him. "Rake the leaves in the front yard before it gets too dark. They're so thick the sprinkler can't reach the grass." She waved at him and went off to her study.

"Right," he said, though he didn't think she heard. Then he lay down on the couch and, in seconds, fell fast asleep.

The light had already begun to fade when he awoke an hour later. He gulped the lukewarm lemonade, grabbed a handful of cookies, and went outdoors to find the rake.

Raking leaves was so boring. Any moron could do it. And he wasn't even getting paid. His parents said that running a home was everyone's responsibility. Oh, well. At least it left the mind free to wander. He thought about the twelve-string guitar he wanted, at Grayson's. Maybe he could talk his parents into getting it for Christmas.

He had just begun pushing the raked leaves into a can he'd laid out on the ground when his mother appeared.

"Philip! What in heaven's name are you *doing*?"

"Raking leaves," he said, looking up in surprise.

"I don't believe it! I just don't believe it! Where is your head? Who rakes leaves uphill into a can?"

"What difference does it make?" he shouted.

"But don't you see —"

He threw the rake down and stalked off to the house. Nothing he did seemed to please anyone. Who cared if the leaves were raked uphill or down. If he left them there the wind would sweep them to the next yard, anyway.

"Philip!" his mother shouted at him. "Philip!"

The heck with her. The heck with them all. He kept going until he reached his room. He was sick of them all — Matt, his teachers, Horgan, his mother — everyone! For a second he stood in the middle of his room raging with fury. Then, without thinking, he grabbed up his guitar, ran down the hall and through Matt's room, and let himself out to the backyard. He had to get away. Away from all the criticism. *The shelter.* That's where he'd go. He could close himself off from the whole world down there, underground. Let them worry about *him* for a change.

Chapter 4

Philip lifted the metal cover that formed the door to the shelter, switched on the generator for light and air, and climbed down the ladder. The little room was such a mess! He and Matt should really try to straighten it up one of these days. For now he kicked the loose magazines and books under one of the bunk beds and plopped down on a lower bunk with his guitar.

Maybe he should become a rock musician. His father thought he should go into mathematics, but Philip always felt happiest when he was playing his guitar. Tim thought he had real talent, and Cara said the songs he made up were far better than most of the stuff around. Even Matt admitted he was good. But he also said, "Forget it. The odds are a million to one against you making it."

He plucked a few chords and let his mind float. The bad feelings of just a short while ago began to fade, and soon he was playing and singing some of the songs he'd written.

He'd been lost in the music for perhaps an hour when he heard Matt's voice from above.

"Hey, down there! Anybody home?"

Cara's face smiled down at him through the entrance hole, then disappeared. Soon Matt's legs backed down the ladder. In a moment his brother was standing in the narrow space between the double-decker cots with Cara beside him.

"Truce." Matt held out a granola bar. "Sorry about how I acted at lunchtime." He dropped down on the bed opposite Philip and started to unwrap his candy bar. "Mom says to come up soon. Dad's gonna be late and she's got a class tonight, so we're having dinner early." He nodded at the guitar. "What's that you were playing? Sounded good."

"Play it for us, Phil," Cara said. "What's it called?"

Philip shook his head. The song was about Cara, about lost love. "It's not quite right yet," he said, putting the guitar down. "Did you hear the new Royal Fink album?"

"Hey, come on, Phil. Don't be shy with us," Matt urged.

Philip went to the phonograph. "This is better." He put on the new record and stood back. "Just listen to this guy." He turned up the volume and sat down again, closing his eyes so he wouldn't miss a single note.

The record had been playing only a few minutes when a high-pitched wailing scream sounded over it.

"Hey, what's that?" Cara stood up.

"Is that the air-raid siren?" Matt asked.

"Why would it be going off *now*?" said Philip as he got up to turn the player off.

"It's weird." Cara's eyes widened. "I'm scared!"

"It's probably nothing," Matt said. "You know how it is when we have winds like today. Trees down. Power failures. . . ."

"You think so?"

"Shhh."

Philip looked up as the wailing continued. He remembered how, in elementary school, the teachers used to have them dive under their desks and cover their heads.

"Maybe we should cover our heads," he said lightly. This was stupid. Of course it couldn't be anything serious.

"*Sssh!*"

"If you're so worried, I'll go upstairs and find out —"

"Turkey! If it's for real, that would be the dumbest thing to do. Where's the radio?"

"Damn," Philip said. "I borrowed it last week. It's in my room." He started toward the ladder. "I'll get it."

"No, wait!" Cara clutched at his shirt. "Don't!"

He was halfway up the rungs when a brilliant light nearly blinded him. It lit up the small circle of dark sky outside, penetrating the underground room with icy-white hardness. Philip jumped back, covered his eyes with an arm, and felt the hairs on his body quiver. *Oh, God, what's happening?* he wondered, staring into the terrified eyes of his brother and Cara. Instinctively they rushed together, huddling, arms around each other.

Then, in the eerie brilliance, and before they could think what might be happening, cans flew off the shelves, pelting them like bullets. Part of a wall buckled, and earth spilled into the room. The lights went out. A horrible roar sounded from outside. Philip was thrown against the bunk bed and found himself crushed under the weight of his brother and Cara. He screamed. He heard Cara and Matt's terrified cries and knew it wasn't a dream. His shoulder hurt as if it had been yanked from its socket. His cheek burned, and something dripped onto his neck. Philip was suddenly sure that they were dying.

Perhaps a minute passed, perhaps more, but at last the waves of pressure eased, and he could stand in the darkness without the weight of the others on him. Fierce winds like a hurricane roared outside, and a strange smell filled the air.

"My God, what is it?" Matt muttered. "Listen to it!"

Philip squeezed the painful shoulder and wiped the blood dripping down his face. "You okay?"

"I'm going up!" Matt swept past him.

"Matt, no! Don't leave!" Cara screamed. She stumbled across the can-laden floor after him.

"Where are you going?" Philip cried.

"To close the entrance. You get the flashlight!"

He heard the clank of metal dropping into place as he groped along the beds to the chest of drawers where the flashlight was normally kept. Then he remembered taking it from the drawer last week, playing it against the walls so that it made bright circles of light as he lay on the cot, daydreaming. He swept a hand over the rubble of concrete and dirt on the bed. No flashlight. Candles. Matches. He felt his way back to the dresser.

"For God's sake! Where's the light?" Matt roared.

With fluttering fingers he pulled open the drawers and rummaged blindly among bubble gum wrappers, pencils, paper clips, baseball cards, and other junk until he felt two candles and a partial book of matches. He struck the matches several times before one lit and he could light the candles.

Matt stood at the foot of the ladder, an arm around Cara. Her eyes stared wide and unblinking as he led her to a cot, cleared a space, and sat her down. Then he turned around to look at Philip.

"You okay?" Matt stepped closer and took one of the candles. "You've got a cut on your face! It's bleeding!" He grabbed a handful of tissues from a box on the floor and passed them to his brother.

Philip pressed the tissue against the cheek.

"It's not bad. What happened, Matt? Earthquake?" He didn't think so because of the funny light. "Meteorite?" Let it be anything, he thought, except what he suspected.

Matt darted a glance at Cara, who sat passively staring ahead. "I think — I think it was — a nuclear bomb."

Philip drew in his breath. For a long while neither spoke, then Matt finally said, "What do you think we should do?"

"I don't know!" Philip answered. "Do you think it's war? You think maybe the whole country . . ." He couldn't finish the sentence. And then his heart froze. "Mom! Dad!"

"I'd better go outside. Look around. Find Mom and bring her down here. You stay," Matt said.

"What if there's radiation?"

Matt's eye twitched as it always did when he felt pressured, and he didn't answer. "Where's the flashlight?"

Philip got down on his hands and knees and searched in the rubble of cans, magazines, and dirt until he found it. He stood up and turned on the switch anxiously. What if he used up the batteries last week? He sighed with relief as the light held, and he handed the flashlight to Matt. "Maybe we should all go, stick together."

"No. If I need help I'll be back."

"Be careful, Matt." Philip hugged his brother hard and quick. He wanted to cry. Matt took a deep, scared breath and gave him the candle. Then he turned, climbed the ladder, and lifted the exit cover. There was a clank of metal as the lid fell back into place, then silence. Philip turned to Cara.

She had been sitting with her hands in her lap, staring straight ahead. Now he realized that she must be in shock. In TV movies they always slapped the persons to bring them back. Was that what he should do? He knelt before her and took her hands. "Cara?" he urged. "Come on. Get up. Let's clean this place up."

She stared back at him, not seeming to hear. "Cara!" he said sharply. "Quit it!" He shook her, frightened now by the distant, closed look. And then he slapped her, first on the arm and then on the face.

Her eyes closed and tears came. Philip sat down and drew her close. He smoothed her hair and patted her back, repeating over and over, "It'll be all right. Shhh. It'll be okay."

At last she pulled away and wiped her eyes. Sniffling, she asked, "What happened? Where's Matt?"

"Upstairs, finding out." He hoped Matt wouldn't be gone long. He pictured fallout raining down on him, fires burning, and he wanted his brother. He needed him back. What would he do if he didn't return? Was it possible that the three of them were the only people still alive? He didn't dare pursue such terrible thoughts. He looked around.

"Come on, kid," he said, imitating Matt's self-assured manner. "We'd better try cleaning this mess up. In five minutes Matt will be back with Mom, and you know how she is about neatness."

Cara didn't even smile. She stood up, looked about distractedly, then sat down again. "Who cares? It's all over. I just know it. Some military guy pushed the button, and the whole world's on fire. We'll all die. We'll never get out of here! This'll be our tomb!"

The picture her words made in his head were so frightening that he cried, "Stop it! We don't know that. We don't know anything! Maybe it's just an explosion downtown of some chemical plant. Now get up and help me!" He yanked at her arm. In the candlelight her dirt-streaked face seemed faintly hopeful. "Pick up those cans. I'll see about the break in the wall!"

"But my mother! Jenny!"

"Get busy, Cara. You hear me? Don't think about them! Just do as I said!"

Surprised at his gruffness, she began to pick up the things that had fallen off the storage shelves and put them back. Now and then she'd stop and look toward the ladder. "Where is he? What's happening up there? What if he doesn't get back?"

Philip didn't answer.

After seeing that he could do nothing about the break in the wall, and deciding that it would hold, anyway, he turned to taking inventory. With a kind of feverish energy he made mental notes of everything in the shelter — the contents of his father's fishing box, the number of sleeping bags and backpacks, how much freeze-dried food they had, what canned drinks and other foods. Somehow keeping busy this way helped time pass in a way that seemed purposeful.

When he found the camp stove, he felt a bitter irritation at himself. He didn't even know how the thing worked. Matt or his mother or father had always operated it on camping trips while he'd been off getting water or finding firewood.

"I have to go to the bathroom," Cara whispered apologetically.

"Yeah, yeah. I'll find something." He blushed for them both, aware that in the excitement, he, too, had to relieve himself. "Here . . ." He handed Cara a cooking pot from the camping equipment, then turned away. Whistling to cover any sounds, he moved to the farthest corner of the room and climbed several of the ladder rungs.

Almost an hour had passed since Matt had left. With each minute he felt more anxious. What could be happening? Was his mother all right? What about his father? His office was in Pasadena, ten miles from here. *What if Matt didn't return?*

He couldn't wait any longer, regardless of what Matt had made him promise. He raised the exit cover and looked out.

The wind seemed to have subsided, but the air had an electric kind of smell. He touched a hand tentatively to the nearby blacktop and felt ashes and great heat. Quickly he pulled the hand back, wiping it on his jeans, then climbed another rung so he could see farther. At first all he could make out was the nearby shrubbery and the vague outline of the back of the house. It looked as if lights were on in the house. Lights? No! With horror he realized it wasn't electricity but *fire.*

What should I do? he agonized. *Oh, what should I do? Where's Matt? Why isn't he back?* And then he saw the light wavering unsteadily toward him.

"Matt!" He jumped out of the shelter and ran across the sticky blacktop, sensing the heat through his sneakers.

"She's heavy," Matt panted. "Grab her legs."

Sharing the burden, they hurried back to the shelter. Philip climbed down first, easing his mother through the opening. He took her dead weight into his arms, then backed down the remaining steps. Matt sucked in his breath as if he were crying with exhaustion.

Philip heard the metal cover clang shut just as he dropped his mother onto the cot. She cried out. She was alive! Taking one of the candles, he held it close to her, and his eyes blurred with tears. Her arms and legs, exposed because she'd been wearing shorts and a shirt without sleeves, were red and blistered. Even her face seemed distorted, with brows and lashes gone. She opened her eyes, focused on his face, and smiled a strange grimace of a smile.

"Hello, darling," she whispered. And then, with a sigh, "Thank God you're okay."

Chapter 5

Matt touched his arm and nodded for him to come away. He followed his brother to a corner of the room, leaving Cara offering water to his mother at the bed.

"It's awful out there," Matt whispered, shuddering. He put one hand over his twitching eye, and Philip started when he saw the burns. "I found her in the kitchen, on the floor. She must have been fixing dinner. I think . . . a gas line may have exploded." He paused and shook his head. "I pulled her outside and got the hose but. . . ." His voice quavered. "After a minute or so, the water just stopped coming."

Matt looked so drawn, so *wilted*, as if he no longer had the energy to go on, nor the will. For a moment Philip, too, felt the hopelessness, but then he thought, *We're alive. We're together.* In a voice that projected more calm than he felt, he said, "Get out of those clothes, Matt." He started unbuttoning his brother's shirt. "They may be contaminated. We've got ski pants and stuff in the camping gear, even hiking boots. I'll get them."

"Wait. . . ." Matt put a hand on his arm as he turned away. "What'll we do? She needs help!"

Philip was so used to his brother planning for them, telling him what to think and do next, that for a second he stopped in surprise. Then he said, "We'll get her to the hospital." He watched Matt closely for signs of disapproval.

His brother shook his head and slumped wearily against the wall, covering his eyes with his hands. "There's more."

"What?" he asked sharply.

"I could see L.A., you know? Fires. Everywhere."

Philip sucked in his breath and glanced back to see if Cara heard. "What's happening?" His mother moaned. "We've got to get Mom to a doctor. The hospital's at least a mile. What about the car?"

"No. Driveway's blocked." Matt withdrew his hands; his eyes were bloodshot. "That big pine, the one in the Giaimos' yard, fell. Right across the driveway. It must be like that everywhere. We'd never get through."

Matt slid down the wall and settled on the floor, pressing hands against his stomach, eyes closed. Philip knelt and began unlacing his brother's shoes. "Come on, Matt. Get that shirt off, and let's get rid of these pants. I'll get the clean clothes."

His mind raced as he dumped the contents of the backpack on one of the cots and grabbed at clothes for Matt. What should he do first? He had to get Matt fixed up so they could plan together, work together to help their mother. He'd glanced at her as he passed and had nearly thrown up. Her whole body seemed rigid in some superhuman effort to control pain. She moaned softly. He grabbed the first-aid box and dumped half the contents out in his clumsy fumbling until he found the bottle of painkillers. Was it safe to give one to her? Should she even be given water? Should he be bandaging the burns, putting anything on them? He didn't know the first thing about first aid.

"Give her these," he said, turning to Cara.

"How many?" She took the bottle.

"I don't know. It says two, but that's for headaches and stuff. Three? Four? Give her four."

"I think you're supposed to put ice water on burns," Cara said softly. They gazed at each other for a long second, and Philip's throat contracted. Where would they get ice? The five-gallon jug of water was lukewarm. Where could he get ice?

He turned away, grabbed the boots, wool shirt, and ski pants, and returned to Matt. "Here," he said roughly. "Get into these and I'll get rid of yours." He lifted the heap of clothes gingerly, worrying that Matt might have brought radiation into the room and they'd all be contaminated. Didn't nuclear bombs always radiate people? Quickly he climbed the ladder, lifted the cover, and hurled the clothes as far away as possible.

"I . . . I . . . I think I'm . . ." Matt began to gag.

"Wait, wait! *Don't*!" Philip cried. He ran for the nearest container, meaning to hold it under his brother's chin.

Too late. Matt heaved and retched and spewed up half of his guts, mostly over himself and the floor, as Philip stood over him, revolted and helpless.

"Damn you, Matt!" he cried. "Couldn't you have waited? You've smelled up the whole place." He rushed back to the cot and grabbed an old shirt to wipe up the mess. Cara hurried over with a towel. "*Look* at that. Macaroni and cheese, all over the place. Yuchh!" When he noticed the stricken look on his brother's face, he said, "All right, so it could have been worse." He tried to make light of it, but his heart was pounding. "At least it wasn't spaghetti or pizza."

They'd both eaten the same thing for lunch and *he* wasn't sick. What was wrong with Matt? Was it radiation sickness? Did it come on so soon after exposure? On the other hand, Matt was prone to stomach trouble, wasn't he? What about last week, the night before the chemistry exam, when he'd thrown up most of the night?

"Here, Matt," Cara said. "Rinse your mouth with this." She held a paper cup to Matt's lips. Her hand trembled.

Damn, Philip thought, backing away, wanting to upchuck himself from the smell. *Why'd you go and get sick now? How can you do that to us?* He yanked a plastic bag out of a backpack and dumped the contents of the pot into it along with the foul-smelling clothes he'd used to clean up Matt's mess, then sat on the bed opposite his mother, holding the bag between his legs. *What should I do?* he asked himself silently. *Tell me what to do, God!*

He hardly ever appealed to God, because he wasn't sure he really believed, but sometimes, in emergencies, he made pacts. *Let me win this race and I'll believe in you forever, God. Let me get a good grade and I'll never use your name in vain. Let Mom and Dad love me as much as they love Matt and . . .* Now he thought, *Oh, God, please help us. Save Mom, let Dad be okay . . . make things the way they were. . . .*

But then he knew such thoughts were pointless. If there was really a nuclear war, God would be too busy elsewhere to look in on him. Whatever happened would be up to *him* and Matt, now, not God. With Matt sick, that left only him and Cara. He shivered at the thought.

"Phil" — Cara dropped down on the cot beside him — "he's asleep. I just left him sitting there, but he looks awful. And your Mom. We've got to get help. My parents! My sister! I want to go *home!*" Her voice broke.

"It's dark out! The roads are blocked! I'm not Superman!"

She lowered her head and started to cry quietly.

"I'm sorry." He touched her hand for a second, then jumped to his feet as he thought of the Giaimos. "The neighbors! Maybe Mr. Giaimo can help. Maybe the road's clear below his house."

Wishful thinking, to be sure, but for the moment the bright possibility spurred him to action. Climbing out of the shelter, he envisioned the elderly next-door neighbor greeting him at the door, hearing his plea, rushing to help. He'd drive his car up the road, help him carry out his mother and Matt, and in no time they'd be on their way to the hospital. Why, they might even drop off Cara at her house.

But as soon as he stood upright on the blacktop, he knew he'd been deceiving himself. Matt, the pessimist, had described less horror than now met his eyes. The sky was alight with distant fires. Before him, the house that had been home leaked flames from every opening. The electric smell he'd noticed earlier was now overwhelmed by the acrid smoke of burning things. How long would it be before smoke filled the shelter? He covered his nose and ran to the wall separating their property from the neighbor's. He leaped over the brick, dropped into the yard below, then ran to the back door.

"Mr. Giaimo! Mrs. Giaimo!" he shouted, pounding on the wood. For an instant he visualized the last time he'd seen their neighbor. Some high school kids, celebrating graduation, had TP'd the shrubs and trees on the Giaimo's front lawn. He and Matt had cleared the mess of toilet paper, at their mother's urging, and Mr. Giaimo had brought over a box of his wife's freshly baked *biscotti*.

When there was no response, he ran around to the front door, ringing the bell and banging the door knocker.

"Come on. Come on, oh, please, come on!" he urged aloud, pounding on the door with his fists. He stopped and desperately looked around for another place to go. Across the road was a big field cleared just last week for a new housing project. The trees, which used to block the view into Pasadena, had been taken down, so he could now see where his father would be, except that dark and smoke blocked the normally sparkling view. He turned back, lifted the flashlight, and with only a moment's guilty hesitation, brought it down on the cracked glass panel beside the front door, shattering it with the third blow. Reaching around, he found the knob, opened the door, and went in.

"Mr. Giaimo!" he shouted, feeling like a vandal, ready to explain and apologize, if only they were here. But what if they weren't? Or what if they were here and were hurt? He flipped a switch, but no light came on. He played his beam around the entry hall. Pictures hung askew, and a chair had fallen over. Shards of glass crackled underfoot from a fallen china closet. But, in one corner a grandfather clock still ticked as if the world were normal. He moved on to the next room.

"Mr. Giaimo! Mrs. Giaimo!" he called again and again. His throat was aching with the need to cry.

In the kitchen he found cans and broken dishes all over the counters and floors. He cried out at the sight of the wall phone. He ran to it and plucked the receiver from its hook while he played the light on the wall to find the emergency numbers posted there. With special care he punched the buttons for the fire department, then put the receiver to his ear. The phone was dead.

"No!" he cried aloud. "No!" For a moment he remained motionless in the large, tiled room, biting his thumb and staring at the phone.

The house was so still, so deadly still. He couldn't shake a terribly eerie sense that the Giaimos were dead, that everyone in the world except him and the others in the shelter was dead. His skin crawled with a dread of what he might find in the next room, or the next.

"I don't like this!" he cried. "I don't like this at all!" He thought of running back to the shelter. There, at least, were people, living people. They had food, some water, medical supplies, and even if the ventilation system failed, they might survive. Maybe he should just pack them all up and get out over the mountains. They had camping equipment, food, a stove. But *how*, with his mother the way she was?

He forced himself to move, to go on from room to room, growing more uneasy with each step. *Please, God, I need them. Let them be here, alive,* he begged silently. But the house seemed empty. Aimlessly he retraced his steps, wandering from room to room while trying to think what to do.

If he returned to the shelter he'd have to watch his mother die without being able to do a thing. If he moved on down the block, maybe he could get help, but would there be any? Or would each house have its own problems trying to care for their own wounded, trying to put out their own fires? Was it possible he and Cara could move his mother here, without Matt's help? Would it be safer here than in the shelter?

Just as he was leaving the kitchen, still undecided, he noticed a door slightly ajar. A basement? With new energy he threw open the door and ran down the narrow stairs.

The basement had been partitioned into cubicles. In one he found a workshop; another was storage space. In still another the walls were lined with clay pipes containing bottles.

As he threw open the last door his throat clogged with disappointment. And then he saw them. "Mrs. Giaimo!" In the bright flicker of a large candelabrum he saw the elderly neighbor bent over her husband, who was lying on an old couch. She was almost deaf, and she didn't hear Philip until he was almost upon her. "Oh!" she exclaimed, turning. Her eyes were wide, and her hand clutched at her throat.

He backed away and switched off the flashlight. "I'm sorry. I'm really sorry. I'm so glad to find you!" he babbled. "I was afraid you were . . . You've got to help! My Mom's burned. Matt's sick. We're —"

"Dick's hurt! He broke something. He's in terrible pain. Oh, please do something!"

Do something? What could he do?

He took a deep breath and bent over Mr. Giaimo, touching his forehead the way his mother always touched his when he was sick. His hand came away wet and cold. He shuddered. Was the old man dead? And then he noticed how the leg stuck out at a funny angle. "What happened?"

"He fell, coming down the steps. I didn't want to come down here! I told him!" Mrs. Giaimo cried. "He needs a doctor! Please, child. Go upstairs. There's a phone in the kitchen with Dr. Watkins' name right next to it."

"Lynna! Stop fussing!" Mr. Giaimo's blue eyes opened, and he focused on Philip. "You Matt? Or Philip? Your mother's always . . ." He stopped and took a deep breath.

"Philip."

"Yes, well. I'm sorry your mother — I'd

help if . . ." His eyes closed again, and his forehead beaded with sweat.

"Dick! Dick! We've *got* to get a doctor!" Mrs. Giaimo cried.

Her husband took another deep breath, then opened his eyes again. "Watkins, if he's still alive, will go straight to the hospital. He's not about to make house calls."

Philip started to giggle, unable to stop until Mr. Giaimo put a hand on his arm. "How strong are you, son?"

Philip wiped his eyes. Matt could bench-press sixty pounds; he worked out regularly with weights. Matt was the strong one, not him. He shrugged.

"No matter. We'll soon see." He turned to his wife. "Lynna, be a good girl and get me a nice bottle of Scotch. I'm gonna need it."

"Scotch? What are you talking about? What are you doing, drinking Scotch at a time like this!"

"Lynna. Just do it."

Mrs. Giaimo rose uncertainly. Philip handed her the flashlight, and she left the room, glancing back uneasily. As soon as she had left Mr. Giaimo took Philip's hand and squeezed hard. "I think I've dislocated something. I want you to grab my leg and turn it to the left, as hard and quick as you know how."

Philip tried to pull away, but Mr. Giaimo held his arm.

"Now don't disappoint me, son. From what your mother says, you've got a lot of guts, running like you do and all. The trick is to put out of your mind anything else, just like when you're running. Just don't listen if I cry out. Don't listen to Lynna — she'll scream, for sure. Just grab it and pull." He regarded Philip intently.

Philip's hands began to sweat. He thought of his brother, Cara, and his mother in the shelter. They must be worrying, wondering what had happened to him. He had to get back. "I can't! It'll hurt you!"

"It'll hurt more if you don't. Philip . . ."

He lowered his eyes, then nodded.

"Good. Then maybe *I* can help *you*. Now do it, before Lynna comes back and starts screaming."

Philip took a deep breath, positioned himself to get a firm grip on the oddly turned leg, then closed his eyes. What if he pulled wrong, made it worse? He opened his eyes and focused firmly on the pain-drenched face of the old man.

"Ready?" he asked, heart racing.

"Ready."

"Okay. One . . . two . . . three!"

Chapter 6

"Bring them here," Mr. Giaimo had advised. "Maybe the fire will pass over. The house is brick. We've a new tile roof. If we hole up in the basement, we may get through this awful mess and get help in the morning."

Philip had felt joy and relief that he had someone to tell him what to do next, that they could come back to this safe haven where the grandfather clock still ticked, as if the world were normal.

But now, as he stood at the back door carrying a soaking wet bed sheet that Mr. Giaimo thought might work as a stretcher, he drew back. Outside, the wind roared, and big, red ashes soared by. The dry brush on the hill at the end of the street would surely catch, too, if it hadn't already. Even inside, smoke from the fires burned his nose and eyes.

Mr. Giaimo, who had leaned heavily on Philip as they climbed the basement stairs, now stood beside him. "Go on," he ordered. "Hurry. I'll be waiting when you bring them out."

Holding a wet towel over his nose and mouth, he opened the door and ran. In a moment he was at the wall. He hoisted himself over and raced over the hot, sticky blacktop to the shelter entrance. He pulled at the metal cover, cried out as it seared his hand, then quickly let himself down the ladder into the small room.

"Philip!" Cara rushed to his side. "I was so scared, I thought you might not come back! It's hard to breathe! It's so hot!"

"We're getting out," he announced. "Matt! Matt!" He shook his brother awake. "Come on, get yourself up. We're moving to the Giaimos. How's Mom?" he called over his shoulder to Cara.

Matt rose unsteadily to his feet, then bent over, hands clutching his stomach, and began to retch again.

"Oh, Matt!" Philip turned to Cara. "It's up to us. We've got to get Mom onto this wet sheet and up that ladder. We've got to get out of here." He started to cough. Between spasms he barked, "Matt, come on! Help us!"

"Can't . . ." Matt mumbled, crumbling to the floor again.

"Damn you, get up!" Philip yanked at his arm. "You can throw up at the Giaimos. Get up!"

Slowly his brother forced himself up and

turned bloodshot eyes, barely in focus, on Philip.

"Now help me get Mom on this, then grab an end." If he could keep Matt going maybe he wouldn't notice how awful he felt. "Cara, be ready to pull the sheet under her. Come on, guys. In five minutes we could be sitting in that nice cool basement next door drinking mint juleps."

Cara laughed, then began to cry as she shook out the wet sheet with Philip. He jumped as a burning cinder landed on his shirt and began to burn his shoulder. Smoke was making it hard to breathe. They were all coughing. "Tuck it under her a little," he said in as normal a tone as he could manage. Looking at his unconscious mother, so red and blistered, he fought back a wave of nausea. "Matt, let's get her up. Then Cara can pull the sheet under her."

Gingerly, with Matt at one end and himself on the other, they lifted their mother, and Cara hurriedly pulled the rest of the sheet beneath her.

"Matt!" he cried in sudden anguish. "How do we do this?" When Mr. Giaimo had thrust the sheet at him, he'd said only that it might make a good stretcher. Now he couldn't see how they'd hand her up the ladder in the thing. She'd just slide down to whoever was at the lower end. Should he just forget the sheet and try to carry her?

Matt turned a twisted face, soiled with vomit, to Phil. He clamped a hand over his mouth and began to heave again, then stopped. Weakly he said, "We'll wrap it around her and tie big knots at the ends. You go first. Cara can stay in the middle so she can help support her."

"Right!" Why hadn't he thought of that? Hands trembling, he knotted an end while Cara did the other. Then, following Matt's instructions, he climbed halfway up the ladder. Crouching, he held on to a rung with one hand and with the other reached down for the sheet knot. He could hear the wind raging above. He could feel the heat and smell the smoke. Too late, he realized they should have used whatever water was left to wet themselves.

"Lift!" Matt cried.

"I am!" She was so heavy, and he was so skinny. His strength was in running, not in lifting. His arms were long and thin. A scholar's body, his mother had said once, trying to ease his self-hatred. "So you're not a jock — neither is your father."

"*Lift*!" Matt repeated. "Go on, move! Don't just stand there!"

He was trying, damn it! He clenched his lips, hating his brother. If Matt was so smart, so strong, why wasn't *he* up here? Didn't he realize that he didn't dare let go of the rung to move up, or he'd fall, pulled back by Mom's weight?

"Cara, lift!" Matt commanded.

In the moment that she gave support, Philip was able to pull the knot so that he could grasp the rung, too, freeing his other hand to move up a step. And so, step by agonizing step, he finally reached the top. He knelt on the ground, the heat scorching a hole in his jeans. Trying to keep the sheet from touching the metal rim of the entrance hole — hearing steam hiss each time the wet sheet made contact, he pulled his mother out. At last Cara emerged, and then Matt.

And then the three of them, supporting the heavy, sheet-wrapped burden, ran across the remaining ground to the wall. There Mr. Giaimo waited with a ladder set in place to help hand them down.

The moment Philip reentered the house, he began to breath more easily. In the normalcy of the almost untouched home, the outside horror seemed unreal. In the light of Mr. Giaimo's lantern he saw ornately framed paintings, old-world tapestries, and rosewood cabinets filled with porcelain and china figurines. Here there were people to help; there was a sense of order and calm. He let himself feel the exhaustion he'd denied, wanting only to collapse somewhere and sleep, leaving the others in the capable hands of grown-ups.

They moved immediately to the basement where, in his brief absence, the Giaimos had gathered towels and blankets, bandages and ointments, even cans of juice and a platter of cookies from an upstairs freezer. He helped lower his mother to the old couch, then let Mrs. Giaimo take over. She gently unwrapped the sheet, then gasped and turned away as tears sprang to her eyes. But before long she was applying ice cubes, with Cara's help, to the painful burns.

Philip dropped wearily onto an old packing crate while Matt went off with Mr. Giaimo to find a bathroom. He couldn't believe it; everything seemed so normal. They could live comfortably in a place like this, if it didn't burn. There was food upstairs, and they could bring down mattresses. If they ran out of canned or bottled drinks, they might even drain the hot-water heater. They were probably safe, at least for tonight. As soon as the fire passed over and subsided, he would leave to get help.

"Well," Mr. Giaimo said, hobbling back, flashlight in hand. "Your brother seems pretty sick. We'd better get some fluids in him soon, or he'll become dehydrated, run a fever."

"Mr. Giaimo, what happened? Do you know? We didn't have a radio in the clubhouse."

"A radio, oh, yes! I found one while you were gone. I got so busy, I forgot to see if it works." He dug into his back pocket for a small transistor radio and switched it on.

All Philip heard at first was static. Mr. Giaimo slowly turned the station dial back and forth until finally an indistinct voice came on over the static.

". . . repeat. Stay indoors until further notice. Don't panic. A nuclear bomb has exploded over Los Angeles. We will keep you informed as further information is known.

For now, remain indoors. If you have a basement or windowless room, take shelter there. If you are in an unprotected area, go to the nearest shelter. If neither choice is available, cover broken windows where possible and pull drapes. If your home is on fire, find the nearest cover. Don't panic. Repeat. Stay indoors until further notice. We will keep you informed as more is known."

They listened as the message repeated, adding nothing new, then Mr. Giaimo turned the radio off.

For a long moment they just stared at each other. Philip thought of what he'd read about Hiroshima. But that had been a ten-kiloton bomb. Today, people spoke in terms of one *megaton*, which was fifty to a hundred times the strength of the Hiroshima bomb, even ten to twenty megatons! He shivered. Was the whole country on fire, the whole world? Was this where it would all end, in this basement?

"Philip," Cara called from across the room. "Your mother wants you."

In a dreamlike state he rose and crossed the room to stand before his mother. Her lobster-red color was now a bright pink. She reached a hand out to him. "Hi, honey. . . ."

"Hi, Mom," he said, swallowing tears.

"You burned your shoulder?"

"It's nothing. How do you feel?"

"Fine. Where's Matt?"

"In the bathroom. Got stomach trouble — you know him."

"It was a nuclear bomb, wasn't it?"

Philip nodded.

"Oh, God. . . ."

"It's okay, Mom. We're safe here, and as soon as the fire burns down we'll get you to a hospital." He didn't say how worried he was that the heat might melt the Giaimos' metal garage door, making it impossible to get the car out. Or that the car itself might explode. "Just hold on, Mom."

"Allen . . . oh, God . . . Allen. . . ." She turned her face away.

"Dad will be fine, Mom. I don't think they got it any worse in Pasadena then we did here. We'll try to reach him tomorrow."

"I knew it would happen eventually. I knew it." She spoke with effort. "You can't keep building bombs and more bombs and not expect someone to use them!" She started to cry. Philip squeezed her hand, not knowing what to answer. Then he bent and kissed her swollen face before turning away.

It seemed a long time since Matt had left, so Philip went to find him. He knocked at the bathroom door, calling his brother's name.

"Leave me alone," Matt answered. "Go away!"

"Matt? Can I help? Can I get you anything? Black coffee? Mom says it settles —"

He could hear Matt retching again, then panting and crying. He felt so helpless standing there, listening. If only *he'd* gone out to bring their mother back or at least offered to help. Maybe Matt wouldn't be so sick now.

He waited at the closed door a long while, calling, but all his brother replied was, "Go away. I just want to die!"

"Cara and I will bring down some mattresses," he told Mr. Giaimo. "Matt's gonna need some sleep, and Mrs. Giaimo looks pretty done-in."

"Good idea. I'll give you a hand." The old man rose to his feet, but the bad leg gave under him. Philip helped him up.

"It's okay. We can manage. We'll just slide the mattresses along and push them down the stairs. Cara, let's go."

Cara didn't answer. She just followed him and did what he said. When they had slid three mattresses down the stairs, Philip led the way back to the kitchen and began checking cupboards. "See what's in the fridge, Cara. Get a bag and bring down anything edible. Oh, here's the coffee for Matt."

He turned around to find Cara staring with wide-eyed horror out the window. "Don't . . ." he said. "We're safe here."

"What's happening to my Mom — my sister? Maybe my mother's been burned, and who's helping her? I want to go home!"

"You can't. You know you can't."

"We'll all die. There'll be radiation, and the water will be contaminated, and everything will be burned up, and . . ." she went on, hysterically listing all her fears.

"Cara," Philip said, reaching awkwardly to hold her. "Cara, don't . . . If it was all-out war, I think we'd all be dead." He hadn't realized he'd thought that until the moment he said it. "Come on, don't look. The fire seems worse because of the winds. It'll pass over. . . ." He hurriedly stuffed whatever he thought they might use into a bag and, with one arm around her, guided her back downstairs.

They were greeted by Mr. Giaimo's elated voice. "Come here, listen."

From the radio came a new voice. "Attention. This is your Emergency Broadcasting System. We have just been informed that the nuclear bomb exploded over Los Angeles was of one-megaton strength. We have not assessed the extent of damage yet, but it is known that the explosion occurred approximately one mile above downtown Los Angeles. Experts say there is little hope of survivors within a five-mile radius of ground zero, and that major damage from the blast and fire extends to at least twenty miles. We repeat from earlier broadcasts: Stay indoors until further notice. One moment please. . . ." There was static and unclear voices speaking excitedly in the background, then the announcer came back on. "I have just been informed that the nuclear bomb that destroyed Los Angeles is a singularity. The White House announced that twenty minutes before impact the President received an urgent call on his hot line from Soviet Premier Alexei Antonovich. The Soviet leader said that a nuclear bomb had been accidentally fired and was on its way. He urged the President not to retaliate and to accept the Soviet's heartfelt apologies and regrets. He promised to do all in his power to assist and make amends for this dreadful mistake. We repeat. The drop on Los Angeles was accidental. We are not at war. There is no reason to believe further Soviet missiles will be headed this way. At this time there is no word from the White House as to what steps, if any, this country will take. Repeat. . . ."

"Oh, thank God!" Mrs. Giaimo exclaimed. "Thank God! It's just L.A.!"

"Just a few million people. Thank the Lord for small favors," Mr. Giaimo replied bitterly. "So, it was their mistake! It could just as well have been ours, or Britain's. Nothing's fail-safe!"

"*Would* we retaliate, Mr. Giaimo?" Philip held his breath, waiting for the answer.

The elderly man stared for a long moment at him before saying, "I don't think so. It's up to the President, but I think he's a sensible man."

"Cara, did you hear that? It's just L.A., an accident! That means we'll get help soon. Mom? Did you hear?" Philip ran to his mother's side and repeated what they'd heard, then he rushed to find Matt.

Matt was leaning against the door of the bathroom, too weak to move. Philip put Matt's arm around his shoulder and said, "Lean on me. Come on." Slowly he walked his brother to the other room where he lowered him to one of the mattresses, then found a blanket and covered him. He smelled awful. He looked terrible. Philip wished he could think what to do for him, but the only thing he could think was to get him strong, hot coffee. He'd ask Mr. Giaimo how to get water from the hot-water heater. It was the least he could do, the only thing he could think to do.

How much longer before daylight? How long before it was safe to go out for help? It was already well after midnight. He hadn't had food or water or rest, but he wasn't hungry or thirsty or even tired. Matt had always kidded Philip about his endurance, about his indifference to mess and discomfort, except that he'd always made it sound kind of freakish. Now he was glad he could hang in there and put up with all this mess.

He looked around. Mrs. Giaimo had curled up on one of the mattresses and gone to sleep. Cara lay on the third mattress, staring up at the ceiling. Mr. Giaimo, looking frail and all of his eighty years, huddled in an old easy chair, chin on his chest.

Philip pulled a chair to a spot near his mother and sat down. In the flickering candlelight he watched her, now and then applying water from the melted ice cubes to the most inflamed skin. He had grown used to the smell of smoke, and now of vomit and excrement, and to the faint banshee wails that came from the world outside. He thought of his father, in his lab at the university, or perhaps in his car, on the way home when the bomb dropped. He thought of waking up this morning and looking out over the valley to the green hills across the way. What would it all be like this morning when — if — the smoke cleared?

Chapter 7

He dreamed. In sleep he was back home at the dinner table with his parents and Matt. Matt, as usual, was doing most of the talking. Bored with his brother's voice, with his always knowing everything, having opinions about everything, he asked his father a question. In the dream it wasn't clear what; the words seemed jumbled, unrelated, yet must have had meaning.

The answer, as in life, as in dreams before, was directed to Matt.

When he saw how it was going, he tuned out, diddling with the mashed potatoes on his plate, thinking about his guitar, about Cara, about winning the next track meet.

"You asked a question, and you don't even listen to the answer!" his father exclaimed, bringing him out of his reverie abruptly. "What do you think of Matt's suggestion?"

Three pairs of eyes focused on him. Three pairs of ears waited for his answer. He smiled with self-consciousness at being so suddenly noticed — and the words that he spoke made no sense at all.

Now, as he awoke, he felt a moment's confusion. Where was he? Why did the place smell so of smoke, even taste of it? Why was he sleeping sitting up?

And then he remembered. He squeezed his arms around his aching middle and looked around. The candles had burned down, and the only light was that of the kerosene lamp. He saw the three mattresses on which lay his brother, Cara, and Mrs. Giaimo. Mr. Giaimo sat curled in a ball on the old stuffed chair. When he raised the lamp to look down on his mother, he saw her eyes following him. "Water . . ." she murmured. She swallowed with difficulty.

He hurried to the table and poured a glass of now tepid water, then gently raised her head and helped her drink. Until that moment he hadn't realized how much hair she had lost. Most of her bangs had been burned to a singed fringe well above her forehead. His stomach churned as he saw the oozing burns on her arms and legs, and his heart ached. He must get help *now*, no matter what it was like outside!

He moved to Matt's side, crouched down, and touched his forehead. Hot. He was terribly hot. When Philip wet a cloth and held it to his brother's face, Matt stirred, opened his eyes, and moaned. "Sorry, Phil, I'm really sorry. Just can't move. . . ."

"It's okay, Matt. Just rest. I'll be back in an hour with the paramedics."

"Mr. Giaimo!" He shook the elderly man awake and whispered, "I'm going. The fires should be over. I'll try to get to the hospital. It's only a little over a mile. I'll bring help."

"Wait, son." Mr. Giaimo rose slowly, testing the strength in his legs. "Try the radio, find out what's new. I'll go check the car. If we can get it out, I'll help you get your mother and Matt in. You drive?"

"Sort of."

"The roads may be blocked, but . . . we'll see." Mr. Giaimo disappeared to see about his car, and Philip turned the radio on low. Cara awoke and sat up. She seemed dazed at first, then reached out to check Matt before joining Philip.

"He's got a fever. How's your mom?"

"Worse. Mr. Giaimo's gone to see about the car. Ssssh!" He held up a hand as a voice came through.

". . . National Guard has been called out, and all state and local agencies not immediately affected by the bomb are mobilizing to assist the victims of this terrible tragedy. Please remain in your home or shelter. Radiation levels are being monitored. Help is on the way. . . ."

"Help is on the way!" Cara repeated joyously.

"On the way could be two — three — maybe even four days, child," Mr. Giaimo said, coming back into the room. "The garage door's stuck, welded to the frame. You'll have to get help without the car."

"I'm going with you," Cara said. "I've got to see about my family!"

"Get yourselves something to eat and drink first. I'll get some old raincoats and boots. You'll want to cover yourselves well."

As Philip gulped the juice and devoured the cheese and bread he'd brought downstairs last night, he realized he hadn't eaten since noon yesterday. Yesterday! How long ago it seemed, and how unimportant all those silly worries over the math test, Matt's impatience with him, displeasing the track coach. Now he thought about his father. He could be buried under a building for all Philip knew. If he was in the car when the blast came, he could have been blown off the freeway. He didn't even want to think about what might be. It was easier to just get out of the house and *do* something.

"Maybe your girlfriend should stay," Mr. Giaimo said when he looked out the front door. The air was gray, as if a great fog had settled over the street, except the fog was smoke.

Philip didn't look at Cara or correct the old man. "Cara? Maybe you *should* stay. I can check your house, tell them you're okay."

"No!" she said without hesitation. "I'm going." She buttoned Mrs. Giaimo's flowered plastic coat around her slender body and tied the sash. "Let's go."

He was glad she was coming. It looked so scary outside. The neighborhood he'd known was transformed into a dark otherworld. Somehow, it wouldn't seem so weird with her along. "We'll be okay," he assured Mr. Giaimo. "Cara's tough. She's on the drill team."

"I'm sure you'll both be fine, but be careful, children. Please be careful." He touched each of them affectionately, then stepped aside.

As they walked to the road, Philip couldn't resist glancing above to where his home should be, but in the smoky air anything more than ten feet away was lost. "Wait here, Cara. I want to see if the house —"

"I go where you go." She took his hand. Cautiously they moved up the street, past the fallen tree, a smoldering skeleton now, to the home his mother and father had bought after years of looking, the home they had put most of their savings into.

Cara gasped. "Oh, Phil. . . ."

Philip swallowed the hard lump in his throat. Hardly anything remained, except part of the outer walls. All his records and baseball cards, all of Matt's books, the piano . . . gone.

"Let's go," he said abruptly. "They're only things." As they moved on down the street a dozen other losses filled his mind — their clothes, everything that made life comfortable, all the family photos. . . . He wiped the back of his hand across his eyes, gripped Cara's hand harder, and turned away.

In the gray gloom, which smelled so strongly of smoke, he glimpsed power poles leaning away from the blast, their wires sagging. The beautiful old trees that had made their street so special, stood bare, skeletons. Across the street the fire hydrant, broken at its base, spouted water. The home downhill from the Giaimo's had burned, and the one beyond that, too. Should they stop and search for survivors, or would their owners have risked fallout and scurried, like rats, to the next home and the next? Where had the fire stopped? Had the whole of La Cañada gone up in flames, except for those rare houses made of brick, roofed with tile, like the Giaimos'?

The road lay thick with cinders and debris, and for a moment Philip worried about radioactivity. But then he had a reassuring thought. When the bomb exploded, the Santa Anas had been blowing, pushing desert air toward the sea. Though the fire at home was due to a gas line bursting, it had been caused by the blast, rather than the direct heat of the explosion. Perhaps, then, all these ashes might be "clean."

"Oh, my God . . ." Cara cried at each new horror. "What could have happened to Mom and Jenny? Hurry!"

After they had walked a block, Cara's hand tightened suddenly in his, then she pointed and shrieked. Before he could stop her, she broke into a run. "Blackie! Blackie!" she cried, falling to her knees before a hill of burned leaves and tree branches, under which he glimpsed a dog's head. "Oh, Blackie. . . ."

Cara's dog had often jumped the six-foot backyard fence and come up to their house looking for her. Philip put a hand to his mouth and stifled the urge to vomit. Blackie's eye sockets were empty, his fur singed.

"Cara, get up!" he cried roughly. He yanked her to her feet, frightened by the wide-eyed horror in her eyes and her awful, nonstop screaming. She tried to pull out of his grasp, but he held her firm, hugging her tight until the screams subsided into sobs.

"Now listen," he said. "I told Mr. Giaimo you were a tough cookie, so don't go making a liar out of me." Tears burned his throat.

She continued to sob, her face in his shoulder, as if she hadn't heard. "Blackie's dead," he went on, "but you're alive, and so am I and Matt and the Giaimos. Now stop that crying and let's go find your family."

The assurance in his tone, an assurance he didn't at all feel, considering what they'd seen so far, seemed to impress Cara. She pulled herself together at last, took one last look at Blackie, then took his hand again. They started off at a quick pace.

Philip urged her along, wondering with each step if they'd find anyone, *anything* else alive. It was so eerily silent for this time of morning. No dogs barking or cars swishing by on the highway. No birds singing on the power lines. He'd seen no one and had been unwilling to investigate an overturned car, thrown up on a blackened lawn.

On Vista del Valle his heart pounded as he heard the first normal sound — a car starting. Cara cried out joyfully and together they ran toward it. Philip recognized the woman at the wheel of the brown Honda as a young mother who often waved to him when he was out running. He ran along beside the car while it rolled backward, pounding on the window. It seemed as if the woman didn't want to hear or see him.

"Please!" he yelled, "we need help!"

At last she stopped and rolled down the window a crack. "What do you want?" She looked years older than he remembered. Her eyes were red and her face was dirty. "I can't help! I've got a house full of strangers, burned, bleeding, sick people. We have no water, no drugs — I have my own to worry about!"

It was then he noticed the small child slumped in the seat beside the woman.

"I'm going to the hospital, too!" he cried. "And Cara needs to get home. It's right on the way. . . ."

The woman considered for only an instant, then rolled up the window and backed away quickly, mumbling something he couldn't hear.

"We'll find others," Philip said. "If *she's* alive, if *her* car works, there'll be others.

Come on." He took Cara's arm and they returned to the road.

Not all the homes along the way had burned. Some had stood up well, with only broken windows and downed trees. He supposed the streets were empty because of radio warnings. The few people he saw carried others or hurried from house to house. At the main road they came upon a tangle of vehicles, trucks, and cars turned every which way, some still smoldering. The road would be impassable for days. If it was this way here, it must be just as bad everywhere. It would take an army of tow trucks to clear the roads so firemen and paramedics could come through. The brown Honda had been abandoned, and the young woman they had last spoken to was running downhill, the child in her arms.

He looked up as he heard the sudden flutter of helicopter blades off in the distance. The powerful, wonderful sound came closer. He scanned the smoke-filled sky but couldn't see anything. Still, the sound raised his hopes. Once he got to the hospital and told them the situation, they'd surely send a helicopter to pick up Mom and Matt.

But Cara chided him when he voiced his hopes. "If *you* can't see *them*, what do you think they can see? They can't land where they can't *see!*"

"I suppose," he answered lamely. She'd used that same tone Matt so often used when Philip had offered some half-baked thought.

"Besides," she added, picking her way over broken glass and roof shingles, "with so many people hurt, it could be days before they'd get to them."

He stopped short. "Then what am I doing going to the hospital? I've got to get back there and find something — I don't know — a sled, a wheelbarrow — *something* to move them in!" His voice broke. "I can't leave my mother there like that. She'll die!" He turned and started to run back in the direction they had come.

"Phil, please wait!" Cara came after him. She grabbed his arm, but he moved on, dragging her. "Please come with me. My mom may be buried under the house. She could be burned just like your mom. Please! I helped you. Help me!"

"I can't, Cara. I want to, but I can't," he said, still moving.

"It's only another block! *Please!*" She began to cry. "If you come with me now, I'll go back with you — if my mom and Jenny are okay. . . ." She began hitting him. "*Stop!* I can't stand it! Don't you realize? My *Dad* works *downtown!* All I've got is Mom and Jenny!"

He paused, torn between her fears and his own family's needs. They were wasting so much time! How much longer could his mother go without medical help? And Matt. And what about *his* father! He thought about the young mother they'd met. She'd known her priorities. When the world was coming to an end, you didn't waste time on others. It was me first. Mine first!

"Damn!" he said, turning back. "All right! Come on!" He began leaping over the obstacle course of debris with Cara following. He supposed he was making a stupid decision again, that Matt wouldn't go off on a tangent like this in the same situation. . . . Angry with himself, he yelled back at Cara. "Damn it! Come on!"

In a few minutes they managed to reach the back of Cara's home by detouring around downed trees, a power line that was sparking, and the ever-present soot and debris and burning embers. But her house was standing.

Cara came up behind him, panting. She pounded on the door, screaming, "Mama, Mama! Open up!"

There was no answer. Philip moved around the house until he found a low window, its glass broken, through which they could enter. It was the dining room. The crystal chandelier lay in shards all around the room, and the china closet's contents littered the dining table and floor. Cara cried out, then hurried on to the kitchen, calling.

The kitchen, too, was a shambles, with most of the dishes and cans from cabinets strewn all over the floor. "Oh!" Cara cried. "Where are they?" But a tour of all the rooms turned up no one.

"Would she have gone somewhere? Left a note?" Philip asked.

"Yes, maybe. But where?" They searched

in the kitchen rubble, kicking at the layers of mess until Philip found a sheet of paper, half-buried. He picked it up and handed it to Cara.

"They're in Burbank!" she exclaimed, laughing and crying at the same time. "With my grandmother! Look! Mom says to warm up the cheese enchiladas in the fridge for supper. She'll be back about eight!" Biting her lip anxiously, she looked at Philip. "Is Burbank . . . how far is it from downtown?"

"Pretty far," Philip said, though he didn't really know. "Farther than *we* were from ground zero."

"Oh! Thank God!" Cara's face broke into a brilliant smile. "Now I feel better. Let's go! Now I can stay with you and Matt and help your mom."

They were on their way back for only a few minutes when it seemed as if the number of people in the streets had suddenly doubled, even tripled. Most of the people outdoors looked hurt or ill. They stumbled along down-hill or were helped by others. Philip stopped a boy he recognized from high school. "What's up? Any news?"

The boy was trying to maneuver a bicycle, on which his sister precariously perched, through a maze of debris. "Radio says the radiation danger isn't great. It's up high and drifting over the coastal cities. But they figure once the winds quit, that radiation cloud's gonna drift right back. Five, six days, the fallout's gonna start coming down good.

I gotta get Marcie to a hospital." He pushed on.

"Yeah."

Philip quickened his pace, pulling Cara along. He had to get his mother and Matt to help fast. If the wounded started moving out of their shelters to the hospitals, pretty soon there'd be wall-to-wall bodies there. Then what kind of care could they get?

Chapter 8

"We could make a stretcher," Mr. Giaimo said, already on his feet and hobbling out of the room. "I was a builder, you know. Got all sorts of things laying around from old jobs."

Philip had suggested using a wheelbarrow to carry his mother, but the thought of her falling out onto the dirt and broken glass along the way made him discard that idea even as he voiced it. Did the Giaimos have a patio lounge? Maybe they could roll it downhill to the hospital. But even that idea wouldn't work. She'd be jostled and bumped. She'd be a mass of ooze and pain by the time they got her a block away.

"A stretcher. Good idea."

It was Matt's voice behind him, weak but firm. He'd stopped vomiting during the night, and Mrs. Giaimo's care — aspirin and forced liquid — had brought his fever down.

"How do you feel, Matt?" Philip asked.

"Like a wet rag." Matt forced a weak smile. "Don't worry. I don't think it's radiation. Probably that nervous stomach of mine, or I'd still be vomiting." He gave an embarrassed laugh.

"He shouldn't be out of bed," Mrs. Giaimo said. "He's dehydrated. That fever won't stay down."

Mr. Giaimo sighed. "Lynna, Lynna. Why don't you see what the children need to take with them?" He turned to Philip. "Boys, give me a hand here, will you? These poles will do fine."

Philip helped pull two eight-foot-long poles from under a pile of lumber stacked on a shelf. "Put them on that workbench. Now where's that old tarp?" Mr. Giaimo beamed the flashlight along the various shelves of building materials until he found what he wanted. "There. Take that down. It's heavy — there's probably twenty to thirty feet of the stuff — but that will be just the ticket."

Philip couldn't quite visualize how the boards and rods and tarp would all go together to make a stretcher, but he kept quiet, unwilling to show his ignorance. He saw the light of comprehension already dawning in his brother's eyes as they unrolled the unwieldy canvas. "Oh, I get it," Matt said. "You'll cut the tarp so you have the grommets on one side to tie to one of the rods. But what about the other side? How will you secure that? Got a stapling gun?"

"Wish I did."

"Then how? Oh! You'll roll the tarp over the rod then nail those boards together with the tarp between." Matt's hands trembled, and perspiration dropped down one cheek.

"Exactly," Mr. Giaimo said.

Exactly, Philip thought. It was so obvious, but *he* hadn't been able to see it.

The cutting of the tarp took the longest time, but once done, Philip and Matt went at tying twine through the grommets while Mr. Giaimo hammered the wood holding the tarp on the opposite side. Suddenly the emergency broadcast station began sending again. They all looked up.

"Attention. Attention," the voice said. "Residents of coastal areas from Santa Barbara south to La Jolla are urged to remain indoors until further notice. Foothill residents may leave their shelters, as the atomic cloud is moving westward. Please help your neighbors. State and federal assistance is being mobilized, but it may be forty-eight hours or longer before it reaches your community. Damage is extensive. Roads and airfields are blocked or damaged. Until help comes please make every effort to put out your own fires and remove trees or other obstacles from roadways. Stay tuned for further information and instructions."

"I guess we were lucky," Matt said softly. "The winds must be carrying that atomic cloud out to sea. What happens, I wonder, when the Santa Anas stop blowing?"

Mr. Giaimo put his hammer down. "Just take it a minute at a time, son. That's all any of us can do. For now — we've made a decent enough stretcher. Let's see how we can move your dear mother without hurting her too much. Then you can be on your way."

At last they stood together at the Giaimos' front door, ready to leave. Mrs. Giaimo hugged each of them as if she thought she'd never see them again, tears in her eyes. "If you can, let us know how it goes," Mr. Giaimo said to Philip. "Take good care of yourselves." He put an arm around his wife and stepped aside.

Philip took the lead, a stretcher pole in each hand. Behind him his mother lay, covered by a clean white sheet on the canvas. Cara and Matt each held one of the back poles. But within a block Matt began to falter.

"Cara," Philip called. "Give Matt a rest. Can you take the full load?"

"I'll try." She grasped both rods, but the weight was more than expected, and she nearly fell.

"Matt, come up here and hang onto me," Philip said. He spoke irritably. His own arms ached from the weight, and he couldn't see how Cara would hold out all the way. He scanned the debris-filled streets for help, but the people outdoors seemed busy with their own.

"It's easy, Cara," he said, trying to sound lighthearted. "Horgan makes us go beyond what we think we can all the time. When I'm running, and I think I can't go another step, I tell myself — just ten more, then just nine more, then just eight more."

Cara stumbled, nearly dropping her end of the stretcher. Philip called out to her sharply. "I can't!" she protested, tears in her eyes. "My arms are shaking. . . ."

"Come on," he urged. "Just tune it out. I'll talk to you. You know Mr. Giaimo? Well, Mom says he's eighty! Spry as a puppy, too. Last week he was up on our roof putting a screen in the chimney." As he maneuvered around a downed telephone pole, he took in the scene ahead. So many fallen trees, so many smoldering homes. So many people looking dazed, carrying belongings out of their homes, wandering around aimlessly. He gazed skyward as he heard what sounded like a squadron of helicopters overhead, but he still could see nothing.

Matt leaned heavily on him, his face unnaturally pale, and his mother whimpered from time to time as they moved too roughly. He welcomed the sound, though each time it hurt like a blow to the stomach. It meant she was still alive. Everything depended on him now. He had to keep Matt going, and Cara.

"Hey, you should hear the funny story Mr. Giaimo told Mom," he said, hoping to get Cara's mind off her pain. "There's this couple, married seventy-five years, goes to a judge to ask for a divorce. 'She's impossible,' he says, and he gives all these reasons why he hates her. And she says, 'He's impossible,' and goes on and on about him. 'If you hated each other so much all these years, why did you wait so long to get a divorce?' the judge asks. 'We stayed together for the sake of the kids, and now they're all dead,' the couple says.

When Cara didn't even smile, he said, "You know — there's one good thing you can say about this nuclear holocaust. . . ." He paused. "Cara, you're supposed to ask me *what*."

"What?" Cara asked weakly.

Good, she's listening, he thought. He tried to readjust his hold on the stretcher without jarring his mother. "After this, we won't need lights at night. People will glow in the dark."

He heard a weak titter from Cara and glanced back. She was very near exhaustion, and they were still blocks from the hospital. He stopped near a home relatively undamaged by the blast or fire, set the stretcher carefully on the ground, and unhooked a canteen of water from his jeans. "Drink, Matt," he urged, "and here's more aspirin." He shook three pills into his brother's trembling hand and held the canteen to his lips. Glassy-eyed, Matt watched him without interest.

"Turkey," Philip chided as he touched his brother's hot forehead. A chill of fear raced through him. He spilled some of the precious water into his hand and patted it on his brother's face. "You're just trying to get out of the heavy work, that's all." Matt didn't answer, and Philip's heart contracted. Normally Matt would never let him get away with a taunt like that. As much as he used to hate the put-downs, he'd give anything for one now, no matter how harsh.

"Okay, let's get going," he said gruffly. "Cara? Lift!" He sifted through his repertoire of jokes and funny stories and began telling another, but Cara wasn't listening.

Matt's weight on him, plus the weight of his mother, made his arms feel like they were being torn from their sockets. He fixed his eyes on the ground and trudged along, gritting his teeth.

"I can't . . . I can't anymore," Cara cried in anguish as they came in sight of the Church of the Lighted Window.

"Just a little farther. Just ten more steps. . . ."

Cara shook her head and slowly dropped to her knees, lowering her end to the ground. She started to cry quietly. "I can't even lift my arms. Look."

"Stay here. I'll see if I can get help from the church." He crouched beside his mother. "Mom? You okay?" She barely nodded, eyes closed. "I'll get you there, don't worry." His throat knotted. Then he sprinted around the overturned cars to the church across the street.

The church lawn was covered with bodies, bodies on blankets, on sheets, even on newspapers. People moaned and cried out, begging for water. He hated to look. Some were burned, others cut, bleeding, limbs broken or torn away. The smell of smoke, now mixed with that of vomit and worse, made his stomach lurch. He tugged at a woman rushing by, carrying a heavy bucket in one hand and an armload of towels in the other. "Excuse me, can anyone help me? My mother is across the street on a stretcher. I need someone to help carry her to the hospital."

"We haven't enough help ourselves." The woman dropped some towels beside one of the bodies and moved on. "I'm sorry. Bring her here if you can."

"But she needs a doctor!"

"They all do! Please, out of the way!"

He darted around bodies to the open church door. Inside, it was even more crowded, and those helping the wounded looked as disheveled and harried as if they'd been at it nonstop for days. "Mister — excuse me!" he said, stopping a man. "I need help. My mother —" His voice cracked, and he felt tears starting. The man put a hand on his shoulder. "I know, son." He gestured to the madhouse around him. "We haven't enough bandages or medicine or anything. Until relief comes, we can't do much. Bring her here and we'll do what we can."

As the man turned to someone else, Philip realized that it was hopeless. What was one mother when there were hundreds, thousands of mothers and fathers and children hurt? He gulped down the tears and turned back to the door. With Matt so sick, with Cara shaking with fatigue, it was up to him.

He hurried back across the street. Cara,

bent over Matt, looked up. "He passed out!" she exclaimed.

"Matt! Matt!" He shook his brother, then stood back and cried, "Oh, God! What should I do?" He looked around wildly. He couldn't leave his brother here alone. But if Cara stayed behind, who'd help carry the stretcher? *What should he do?*

"I've got to get Mom to the hospital," he cried. "There's no other way. They're full-up at the church, and they have practically no supplies. I've just got to do it. It's her only chance."

"How? She weighs as much as you do," Cara said.

He began circling the stretcher, trying to figure out where to lift his mother so it would hurt her as little as possible. Cara plucked at his sleeve. "Philip! You couldn't!"

He shook her off. "See what you can do to get Matt to the church. Maybe someone there can help him. I'll try to get back to you once I get help for Mom. But if Matt feels better, come on to the hospital." He draped the white sheet, now dirty with soot and ashes, around his mother and lifted her carefully. She cried out as he nearly toppled backward, then she continued to whimper. Clenching his teeth, he tottered ahead a few steps and stopped, then stumbled on across the broad boulevard strewn with debris, swaying and reeling, on and on down the road leading to the hospital.

He staggered into the hospital parking lot carrying his mother's limp body. It felt as if she were glued to his arms. His heart pounded and his chest burned. Sweat trickled down his face, down his neck, down his arms and legs. His breath whistled with each step. He had barely winked during the entire walk, putting all his concentration on reaching the next house, and then the next, and on and on. Finally he saw the hospital. Standing. Not destroyed. With a yelp of hope he had run the last steps and stood in the parking lot with tears streaming down his eyes, his mother's limp body still in his arms.

"Let me help you there."

He turned to the gentle voice, almost not understanding.

"Here, son, give her to me."

He couldn't. "She needs a doctor. . . ."

"Yes, of course. Set her down there on that mat. We'll get to her as soon as possible."

He followed meekly, eyes fixed on the back of the man with the kind voice. When they got to a small mat, he set his mother down carefully. Her cry of pain was a knife in his heart. When she was settled, he lifted her head and shakily offered her water from his canteen. He must see that his mother got a doctor, then he'd go back and find Cara and Matt. For the first time he lifted his eyes from his mother and took in the crowded parking lot. The scene was even more horrible than that on the lawn of the church. He nearly gagged. Speechless, he dropped to the ground beside his mother, buried his face in his hands, and burst out crying.

Chapter 9

"Phil . . . Phil. . . ."

He started at the sound of his mother's
voice and looked up through eyes blurred
with tears. Slowly she raised an arm and let
her fingers brush his cheek before the arm
fell back.

"Find . . . Allen. . . ." Her tongue licked dry,
swollen lips.

He rose unsteadily to his feet. Find Dad.
But how? There was no way to get across the
arroyo separating La Cañada from Pasadena
— no way without wings. With all the trees
and brush growing there, the arroyo had to
be ablaze.

What would Matt do in this situation? He
always seemed to know the best thing to do.
Maybe he should go back, ask Matt, do whatever he said. *No.* He had to find a doctor first
for his mother. He gazed around in a kind of
numb stupor, unable to take in what he saw.

The parking lot looked like a battlefield full
of the wounded and dying. Bodies lay every

which way on the ground, in every inch of space, yet more and more came with each minute. They staggered up the hill from the direction of Los Angeles, arms held far away from their bodies, eyes unseeing, bumping into anything in the way, falling. Where were the nurses, the doctors? He stepped over the crying, moaning mass of bodies, some with limbs missing. They were bleeding, oozing, smelling of. . . . He put his hands to his face and swallowed the bile that rose to his mouth.

A rough hand grabbed his shirt. "Boy! Help me!"

The hand pulled him firmly toward a woman holding a baby. The woman's mouth was open in a silent scream. Most of her clothes had been burned off. The skin on her face and arms hung loose.

"She's in shock, won't let go," the nurse said. "Come on, dear. Let the baby go so we can help."

The woman didn't seem to hear or understand, and clasped her dead baby in a vise-like grip. The lifeless form resembled something overcooked. Philip turned away and began to heave.

"Stop that," the nurse said quietly. "Now help me. I'll hold her arms and you pry the baby free."

He couldn't bear to touch the charred body, afraid it might disintegrate within his fingers. The smell of burned flesh was overpowering. He continued to gag. He looked away but willed his arms to reach for the baby. He held it at arm's length while the nurse lowered the mother to a mat. She then took the infant from him, wrapped the small form in a towel, and took it away. Philip bent over and threw up.

When he was able to stand upright again, he heard the whirl of helicopter blades nearby and remembered the hospital heliport. Maybe he could get his mother on one of those things, and they'd fly her out to a burn center. He wiped the back of his hand across his mouth and went looking for the nurse, who was crouched now some dozen feet away over a tattered body.

"My mother needs a doctor," he said, pulling at her arm. "She's over there."

"There are no doctors, can't you see? Doctors die, too! I doubt we've got six for the whole hospital!"

He stared at her, unbelieving.

She started moving to the next patient. As she walked she tore a strip from her dress, to use as a tourniquet. "For heaven's sake, don't just stand there. Do something! Go inside and bring me bandages, sheets, water.... Help me!" She turned him around and gave him a push, then hurried off to a small group of nearly naked people limping toward her.

He'd been in the hospital's emergency room just last year when he'd fallen on his hand and dislocated a finger. The place had been almost empty, and in minutes he'd been

X-rayed and attended to. But now the emergency room had no semblance of what he remembered. It was wall-to-wall bodies. There was crying and moaning, and a few people were rushing about.

"Jesus, where are we gonna put them?" an orderly cried as he lifted a burned man onto a gurney.

"More plasma, stat!"

"Someone get down to supply. Bring up more normal saline, more lactated ringers!"

"Take this one away. Who's next?"

"This one won't make it. Put him in the other room. Next!"

"Where's that help they said was coming! Try the phones again!"

"We tried two minutes ago. . . ."

"Try again!"

It was impossible. There were too many injured and dying, with more coming every minute. He stopped a nurse who was carrying an armload of gauze pads and towels. Her uniform was streaked with blood. "Where's the drinking water? I need to bring some outside."

"Back there!" She nodded with a toss of her head and rushed on. He wove between beds and gurneys and people on sheets on the floor amidst broken glass and spilled fluids and vomit and blood.

"Hey, kid!" a man called, "get a broom . . . down the hall . . . and give me a hand here!"

He ignored the man and moved on to where

he saw a nurse kneeling on the ground beside a cardboard box. "Where's the water supply?" he asked.

She looked up sharply. "What for?"

"We need it outside. There are hundreds of people, just like in here."

The nurse began gathering up armloads of plastic bags containing a colorless fluid. "Open that box and bring it with you."

"I need to get water," he persisted, thinking first of his mother.

"For what? The pipes are broken. We can't flush toilets or hose down the mess or clean people up."

"For drinking!" Philip said.

She pushed by him, talking as she moved. "Some bottled water in Supply, if the bottles didn't break; some distilled; a reserve tank on the roof. . . . That's it until help comes. Bring those boxes!"

Philip ripped open two boxes, stacked them on top of each other, and followed the woman back to the most crowded room. Almost immediately the plastic bags were snatched up by nursing staff and set up for IVs. He moved swiftly, obeying orders to bring more boxes, move patients, do this or that. And then he realized that their needs were insatiable, that those outside would be forgotten. And so, without asking permission, he stacked two boxes of the lactated ringers and started outdoors. "Hey, kid! Where you going with that stuff! Come back!" He ignored the voices and left the building.

Outside, he found the nurse who had sent him for water and showed her what he'd brought. Her tired face lit up with joy, and soon the two of them were moving people into new groupings so they could hang the precious bags from car antennas or telephone poles or on anything else still standing aboveground. He made sure his mother was part of the group.

"Now watch," the nurse said to him. "Watch how I do this because you've got to help me do it, too." She fixed the plastic bag on a hook above the patient, unrolled the tubing, then showed him how to find the vein into which the needle had to be placed. "Now you try."

Oh no! he wanted to say, looking down at his mother. How can I? I never did it before! What if I hurt her, miss the vein, go through the vein to the other side? He licked dry lips and felt his heart pounding in his ears. He'd always been squeamish about things like that, like dissecting frogs or picking up injured birds. But looking down at his unconscious mother brought him courage. With shaky fingers he felt for the vein, took a deep breath, and plunged the needle in as he'd been told. His forehead broke out in a cold sweat. Then, letting out his breath, with a big grin he looked up at the nurse and released the rubber tourniquet.

"You'd make a good doctor," the nurse said approvingly. "Now get to the others."

He had no conception of time. It seemed

hours, perhaps even days, but he felt nothing; he wasn't hungry or tired. He just moved mechanically, back and forth, inside the hospital, outside, doing as he was told. They called him "Boy" or "Runner," and he brought supplies up from the basement, moved gurneys, wheeled people or carried them. The smell, the blood, the awful wounds, the constant cries and groans of pain no longer bothered him. He neither felt, nor smelled, nor heard; he was numbed by it all.

At one point, as he was helping an older nurse who seemed on the verge of collapse, he said, "This must be hell, but then why am I here? All I ever did bad was fight with my brother!"

She paused, her hand shaking as she fixed a bandage in place. She looked up at him with dull eyes showing only a glimmer of awareness. And then she covered her face and began laughing. She was shaking and shivering so hard that he reached out a hand to steady her.

Sometime, in what might have been the afternoon, the news spread that radio contact had been made with Goleta police. Goleta, he remembered, was outside Santa Barbara, more than a hundred miles from Los Angeles. Within seconds nearly all the medical help had gathered at the doorway to the radio room, listening.

"National Guard has been called out. They're landing them at Los Alamitos . . ." the indistinct voice announced. "The President has called for help from the armed forces. Hang in there . . . we'll get to you."

"But we need water, antibiotics, all kinds of supplies *now!*" the plaintive voice of the nurse replied. "How long do we wait?"

"We'll air-drop supplies, but with all that smoke, we can't be too precise. Leave the heliport lights on. How long will your auxiliary power last?"

"Two more days — but don't you understand? We've got hundreds, thousands pouring in here! We've only beds for two hundred! They're on the floor, in the hallways, the parking lot! We have no place to put the dead! What about other hospitals? We need doctors, nurses! Our staff has been working nonstop for over twenty-four hours!"

"I'm sorry, nurse. You don't understand. Los Angeles has been *flattened*. Flattened! County General's rubble. The Glendale hospitals are worse off than you. That hill near you protected you from the blast. Don't complain."

Philip shuddered, then glanced at the others in the doorway. He could see on their faces the same shock he felt.

"We'll relay your needs to the La Crescenta sheriff's station. But they've got troubles, too. Each city's got to take care of its own — until we can get to you. Sorry."

"What about *water?*" the nurse repeated. "Our roof tank's nearly empty. We've been out of bottled water for hours. We're down to canned drinks, and almost out of that. . . ."

"Get someone to the fire station. Maybe they can hook up hoses, run it from swimming pools, reservoirs. That's all I can suggest."

"How long?" the nurse asked. "How *long*?"

"Twenty-four, forty-eight hours. Can't say. We should have the roads cleared by then, then we can bring help in and take out your wounded."

"Forty-eight hours . . ." someone whispered beside Philip.

When the nurse didn't answer, the voice came back, exasperated this time. "Listen, lady. We're doing our best. Just picture what we got! Draw a circle fifteen miles out from downtown L.A. and everyone inside that circle, 'ceptin for the lucky ones who got it right away, needs help!

"What's more, that radiation cloud's gonna start dropping stuff right over this whole area in another four days, so we gotta move everybody out, evacuate everybody — sick, wounded — *everybody*. That means millions. Got the picture?"

"Yes. . . ."

"So hang in there. Do your best. That's what we *all* gotta do. We'll get to ya."

When the radio communication ended, the nurse turned to those in the doorway. "You heard!" she said. "We're on our own! Back to work!"

Philip remained in the doorway, hesitating. Then he spoke up. "I'll go to the fire station."

The nurse dropped her voice. "I don't

think it will help. We always have radio contact with the paramedic ambulance, and I can't get through. Maybe the ambulance was out when the blast came, or maybe the radio's smashed or the station was destroyed. I don't know. But I'm thinking that even if you do get there, the few men who haven't rushed home to their own families will be as bogged down with helping the burned and wounded as we are."

"Then what do we do?"

"I don't know. Pool water? Well water?" She paused, and her forehead wrinkled in concentration. "There was a man in yesterday, before the bomb. He had a strained back, could hardly straighten up. We got to talking. Retired, he said, from the Department of Water and Power. He lives just up the block, I think." She moved to her desk and started rummaging through a mess of papers. "Where is it? Yes . . . here!" She held up a sheet triumphantly. "John Billings, on Via Carlotta."

"I know where that is! I run by that street almost every day." He glanced over the nurse's shoulder to see the number. "What do you want me to say?"

"Oh, I don't know!" The nurse gazed around the crowded, frantic room. "Just talk to him! Maybe he knows what to do. Maybe there are reservoirs nearby, and he knows where they are, and he can show you what to do to get that water coming again."

He'd do it, of course, but how could he

leave his mother for so long? He'd put aside extra bags of the lactated ringers for her, hiding them under her arm. But there were thousands of people out there, all begging for IVs. How could he leave his mother and be sure someone wouldn't just tear the lifesaving fluid from her veins to give to their own?

"On one condition," he said, meeting the nurse's eyes defiantly. If she refused he knew he'd go, anyway, because without water, so many more would die besides his mother. He swallowed the fear of her answer and tried to justify asking for preferential treatment. Matt had always scorned people who used their clout to get favors instead of waiting their turn. Philip hated the idea, but felt he had no choice.

The nurse brushed by him. "Oh, please! This is no time for negotiating conditions!" she protested.

He grabbed her arm. "Look! I want to help. I'll do anything. But I can't leave my mom out there on the ground, all alone. Who'll look after her?"

The nurse whirled around. "All right! Bring her inside. I'll find space for her someplace!"

"Where?" he persisted, only slightly relieved. It flashed through his mind that it was just this kind of dogged persistence that always infuriated Matt, and his parents, and others.

"Don't push me!" the nurse said in a warning voice. "I don't *know* where!"

"Will *you* look after her? You, yourself?"

The warning look turned into a scowl. From behind them voices called for more help, more supplies. The nurse turned to the voices without answering. Philip trailed behind, followed her to the supply room, and helped her carry more boxes. "Will you?" he asked again as they left the room together.

"I can't."

"Then will you put her in that back room, the one where they're putting the people who'll be first to get to the burn centers, as soon as the helicopters can land?"

"My God, kid! You're impossible! *I'm coming*!" she shouted to the voice calling. She gave Philip a push. "Get going. It's 832 Via Carlotta. John Billings!"

Philip stood his ground. "The back room?"

"All *right*!" the nurse cried. "All right! Bring your mother in, and somehow we'll find space for her. In the back room!"

He let out his breath in a deep rush. "I'll bring her in right now." He nearly ran from the room, turning only at the last moment to call back over his shoulder, "Thanks."

"Hi, Mom," he said softly, leaning over her. "Mom?"

She moved her lips but no sound came out.

"I'm going to pick you up. It's going to hurt, and I'm sorry, but I have to take you inside."

"Stop that!" he heard someone scream. "Get away from her!"

He glanced up and saw one of the medical aides run along the narrow lanes between bodies toward a man crouched over one of the victims. The man stood, then quickly bent again over the next person before scurrying over the brick wall separating the hospital grounds from the road.

"Did you see that? Did you see that?" the aide screamed, turning to Philip. "He was stealing their gold chains! Their watches! Just yanking them off those poor helpless people. Animals! That's what they've become. Animals!"

Philip stared into the anguished eyes of the speaker, then looked back into his mother's. "Mom," he said again, "can you put your arms around my neck?"

She didn't answer. He reattached the D5W bag to a rod above the gurney he'd managed to acquire. Carefully he lifted his mother, wincing at her obvious pain. He laid her on the clean sheet. The woman on the ground nearest them lay with skin hanging in rags from her arms. The man next to her stared up at the sky, even though his eyes were gone from their sockets. Philip shuddered and wiped away tears, then took a deep breath. He pushed the gurney toward the emergency room door. His mother's eyes opened. Through tears he smiled down at her.

"Allen . . ." she mumbled.

"Don't worry, Mom . . . I'll find him," he promised.

Chapter 10

He took a deep breath as he left the hospital by way of the body-strewn parking lot. The air was still smoky. He heard helicopter activity far off. Cries for help, screams, sobbing, hysterical babbling, and the stench of something other than smoke assailed his senses.

For the first time in almost twelve hours he thought of Matt and Cara, wondering why they hadn't come to the hospital yet. Could Matt be too sick? Could he be. . . . ? He stopped as his legs started to shake, a quivering that invaded his entire body. Maybe he should forget everything, except getting to the church to find out!

Wait. Slow down. Don't panic, he said to himself. Maybe there's another reason. Maybe they're still at the church because they're helping out, same as I am.

That sounded plausible, and it quieted him. He began to move again through the mass of bodies. If he could find that DWP engineer and help get water to the hospital somehow, that could affect a whole lot of lives.

He hoisted himself up to the brick wall edging the hospital grounds and looked down. The road from Glendale and from Los Angeles seeemed alive, a black ribbon of movement. The human stream, like an army of ants, curled uphill around stalled or overturned vehicles and detoured around the rubble of buildings. A hum rose to his ears, sending a shiver down his spine. Eerie. There were none of the suburban sounds so typical of this time of day — crickets and birds, auto traffic, children skateboarding down the hill. Only the steady drone of tramping feet and a windlike moan.

At closer range he saw individuals. Mothers, fathers, even children were carrying or leading their wounded, themselves wounded, burned, and exhausted. He wanted to rush down and pick up the child screaming for its mother, to rescue the old lady falling beneath the tight march of feet. But the mob moved on, pulling the weak and fallen with them.

Why? Why? he asked himself. It all seemed so dumb! Philip thought of the millions spent each year to keep people alive a bit longer; what did it mean next to the *billions* spent to develop weapons that could kill them faster? If it wasn't so horrible it would be funny. He closed his eyes for a moment and sucked in his breath. He needed to shut off his senses and turn off his mind so that the smells and sights of death and dying wouldn't hurt so much.

It seemed so hopeless. Thousands upon thousands of people trampled over each other, rushing in frantic haste to get away. To where? The mountains, with the desert beyond? How would they survive? They were so crazed, so desperate and sick and ill-equipped. How would they ever make it through forty miles of mountains?

He turned away. In the few moments he had spent watching the scene below he had reached a decision to avoid the mobbed road; it was too slow and dangerous. He'd have to get to Via Carlotta some other way. He looked back at the hills behind him. He could reach the street where the water and power man lived by going that way. And from up high he should be able to pinpoint the swimming pools nearest the hospital.

He dropped to the ground and started up the slope, which had once been covered with brush and was now scorched and mostly bare. The drone of distant aircraft made him look up to the murky sky. Off to the east, from where the sound came, he saw white dots falling. Parachutes! He scrambled on over the difficult terrain, glancing up from time to time. It would be a long while before help would reach them.

He dropped down from the hills near the first home that led to the housing tract and from there to Via Carlotta. It was an old house, and its top lay in rubble halfway down the street while its lower half tilted in the same direction. He bypassed the debris and was about to take a shortcut between two still-smoldering homes when he heard the eerie howl of a coyote. He stopped. Sweat rushed to his skin. Coyotes lived throughout these hills though he'd never seen one. He'd only heard them late at night, yipping and howling. They came out of the hills for food and water, especially in early evening. He'd heard stories of packs ganging up on helpless animals and even small children. The Giaimos had had a cat carried off by a coyote right before Mrs. Giaimo's eyes as she stood screaming for help.

He decided to detour. No sense in looking for trouble. And then he heard a dog's hysterical bark and the cry of a child. He hesitated, then immediately reversed his direction.

He saw the coyote first. From the rear, the yellow-gray fur looked mangy. Portions of skin showed through where fur had burned away. The animal stood with its forefeet resting on its prey.

When Philip drew closer, the animal turned, bared its teeth, but held its ground. What he saw brought bile to his throat. Someone lay beneath the coyote, covered with blood and flies, trapped by a fallen tree. He began to retch, but then he saw the child. No more than two years old, the little girl lay huddled on the ground on what must once have been a pleasant patio with a view of the valley. Guarding her was a small brown-and-white dog. The dog barked furiously, advancing and retreating, warning, threatening, but not attacking. The child screamed. Her eyes were wide with terror as she reached her hands out to Philip.

Angry and repulsed, he grabbed up the nearest object that could serve as a club and turned on the coyote. His heart was pounding, and strange, strangled sounds came from somewhere deep inside him. He advanced. "Git! Scram! Git, you . . . you . . . Leave her alone!" he screamed. He felt as if he could smash the animal, murder it, bash it to pieces.

The coyote slunk away, loping off to a safe distance where it stopped and looked back.

The child's cries brought Philip back to sanity. He threw down the club and rushed to her. Dirty, tear-streaked, she had burns on her chubby arms and legs. He picked her up gingerly and hugged her to him. The mother was dead; of that he was sure. Without a backward glance he turned and ran, the dog at his heels.

The more destruction he saw, the more anxious he became. So many of the homes were charred rubble. Any swimming pools he saw were so littered, he couldn't believe the water was drinkable. What if the water and power engineer's home had also burned? What if he was dead? Or gone, one of the thousands escaping to the hills?

But the homes on Via Carlotta had suffered

less than others, he discovered with relief. Perhaps it was because of their tile roofs. For the first time he came upon families leaving. They pushed wheelbarrows full of belongings, their children tied by lines to their wrists. He asked for water for the child. "We haven't enough for our own," people said.

He knocked fearfully on the door of 832 Via Carlotta, a door that was charred but still standing, and waited. As he nuzzled his chin in the baby's soft hair, he realized that its diapers were wet and full. How long had the child been outdoors without food or water, waiting for its mother to move? The bomb had exploded yesterday about this time. If he hadn't come, would the coyote have, gone after her, too?

After a time he heard footsteps, then a woman's voice, high-pitched with fear, called to him through the closed door. "Go away! We'll shoot! We've got a gun!"

Philip backed off, the sweat rising suddenly to his forehead. Were they crazy in there? Would she actually shoot?

"I'm looking for Mr. Billings!" he called back, a tremor in his voice. "I'm from the hospital. Is he there?"

He heard a lock turn, and then the door opened only the width of a chain. He placed himself so he could be seen, though he couldn't see inside the darkened home. "What do you want with John?"

"Please, open the door. Let me talk to him.

I need his help to get water. The pipes broke, and people need water — and I've got this baby who needs care."

"Wait!" The door closed and the footsteps receded. Philip shifted the sobbing child so that her head lay on his shoulder. He put an ear to the door and heard voices mumbling in the background, then two sets of footsteps returned. The chain was removed and at last the door opened.

Before him, holding a gun that was leveled at his middle, stood a plump woman in her sixties, wearing a flowered housedress. Just behind her stood a tall, slender man on crutches. The woman glanced around anxiously as if suspecting that Philip had a dozen accomplices who might dart out of hiding and storm the house.

He'd never faced a gun before. He stepped back, trembling, and then suddenly the whole scene seemed ridiculous. This old woman could be Grandma Singer. How could she consider him a threat? He shivered until he nearly wet his pants, and then suddenly he was giggling, laughing until tears came.

"Let him in, Dorothy. It's okay," the man said. Then to Philip, "Come in, son."

"The baby hasn't had food or water since the bomb, I think," Philip said when he regained control. "I don't know anything about babies. Could you — do you think. . . . ?" He left the sentence unfinished.

Mrs. Billings handed the gun to her husband and reached for the child. She cradled it in her arms and began to make sympathetic cooing sounds. Relieved, Philip waited as the door locks and chains were replaced.

"I'm John Billings," the tall man on crutches said. "You're...."

"Philip Singer."

"Okay, Philip. Follow me."

Philip followed the man through several badly damaged rooms whose contents were strewn about and whose walls were cracked, to a small room that must have served as a den. Its windows had been boarded up, and the room was lit by candles.

The retired engineer lowered himself cautiously into a hard-backed chair. Philip brushed off his filthy jeans, knowing it would do no good, and sat on the couch opposite.

"Sorry about the greeting," Mr. Billings said, "but it's an insane world. This morning three men with guns came down the street and broke into every home. They raped and killed a woman two doors down. They'll steal anything — they're not just after food."

"People are evacuating," Philip reported. "Verdugo Road is mobbed. I haven't heard a radio report. Are they telling people to leave?"

"The army should have the roads cleared in another twenty-four to thirty-six hours, then they'll start evacuating. But most people won't wait, they're too afraid of radiation, although we're told that isn't a danger yet. I'm staying." He nodded at his crutches.

"Couldn't get far with these, anyway. Now, tell me what you want."

Philip explained how things were at the hospital and told how he had come to this home because the nurse had remembered that Mr. Billings had worked for DWP. "So I guess what I'm hoping is that you'll know the location of the nearest wells supplying the hospital and you'll be able to get us some water," Philip finished. He took in the engineer's pained expression as he shifted slightly in his chair and remembered about the strained back. "Or tell *me* what to do to get the water flowing," he added.

"It's not as simple as that," Mr. Billings said, rubbing his thinning gray hair. "Do you know anything about the water system, how it works?"

Philip's face grew warm. If Matt had been here he would know. Matt knew such things. But it was different for him. He was funny about learning — he picked up some things and not others. Like the way he could draw maps of every continent, country, and even every island in the world. But he couldn't figure out how to change a bike tire. "No, sir. I'm sorry, I don't," he said.

"Well, I'll explain it, then maybe together we can figure out what to do."

Water, the engineer said, came from two sources. Local wells, deep in the ground, and from the Colorado River, some distance away. It was the local well water that fed most of the city. Pumped from underground through pipes, it went first to reservoirs spotted around the city. From there the water was again pumped to city streets and individual homes. If a pipe broke on any given street or a hydrant was knocked over, the water and power people could shut off the flow to that one block.

"There are shut-off valves at the wells to stop flow into the reservoirs, and at the reservoirs to stop the flow into the pipes going to homes. Each reservoir holds about a three-day supply of water."

"When I left my block this morning," Philip said, "all the hydrants were spouting water. I wondered how long that would go on until all the water was gone."

"The reservoirs are probably empty or close to it, unless the valves at the wells were still open."

"Do you know where the wells are? Could you get to them and divert that water?"

He shook his head. "I know where every well is in this city, but it wouldn't do any good. First, we'd have to turn off the flow to the reservoirs. Those valves are deep, maybe two hundred feet down. You need special turnoff rods to reach them and strong men to turn those rods." He shook his head again. "Even if we had the manpower, we can't get those rods. They're on the tank trucks, which could be in the DWP yard in Pasadena, or anywhere in between here and there." He scratched his head. "But even if we could stop the flow, we couldn't pump it up. The pump is run electrically."

"And the power's out," Philip said.

"And is likely to be for weeks."

"What about swimming pool water, Mr. Billings?"

"I don't know. Normally it's drinkable, but now with all the debris and ash — I don't know."

"The hospital has contact with Goleta. Maybe they could find out how to purify it, unless the radiation —"

"Yes, the radiation. I don't know. They said it was an air burst. Not so much radiation at first, but in four or five days . . . I don't know, maybe it would be all right."

"How? How do we pump it? And how do we get it all the way to the hospital?"

Mr. Billings lifted himself from the chair just as his wife came to the door. "That's a sweet little baby, John. Poor thing. I cleaned her up as best I could and gave her some milk. She's sleeping now. And that poor dog. He drank so much water I thought he'd burst." She looked at Philip. "Would you like something to eat, young man?"

His stomach rumbled at the mention of food. "Anything would be great. Thanks." He turned back to Mr. Billings. "The hospital's at least five blocks from here, sir. We can't get hose from the fire department. What are we going to do?"

Chapter 11

Within an hour he left the house to scout
the position of pools nearest the hospital.
It was late afternoon. What little light the
sun had offered through its lid of smoke was
now disappearing. Soon it would be really
dark. What then?

There were no streetlights to expose the
dangers underfoot or lurking in the shadows,
and no comforting glow of home lamps. It
would be scary to be outdoors, even with a
flashlight.

He tried not to let himself imagine what
might happen in the dark. So many people
owned guns these days; not just the crim-
inals but good guys, too. Poking around
people's property, as he'd be doing, he could
be taken for an intruder. Before he could
identify himself, someone might. . . .

If only Matt was here. Somehow, with
Matt by his side, Philip would feel safer. If
only things were as they used to be. Around
this time of evening they'd usually be in his

room or Matt's. They'd smell dinner cooking. They'd be talking about school and other things, like if there was a God, and if it was possible to have lived before. And then they'd go down to dinner, and it was a good feeling to be together. And when they asked his father what he did at his office all day, he'd say with a straight face, "I play *tiddly-winks....*"

But those times were gone, maybe forever.

As he crossed a road, eyes scanning each house or the remains of one, he began to feel like he was in a graveyard. How many people lay under those ruins? Maybe some were still alive. Who would help them? Had those who had survived taken off for the mountains?

The dog startled him, appearing suddenly by his side as he climbed over a pile of brick into what was once a garden. It was the small brown-and-white scottie he'd found protecting the little girl.

"Go home!" he called sharply. "Go on! Home!" He had enough problems without a dog to worry about, too. He threw a stone at the dog, deliberately missing it.

The dog moved closer. Its fur-tattered tail wagged uncertainly.

When Philip bent to pick him up and turn him around, the dog yipped in pain and jumped from his hands, scurrying away to a safe distance where it stretched back its head to lick its wounds.

"I'm sorry, dog," he said. "But why do you

want to come with me when you could be comfortable and safe at the Billings'!" His throat tightened. It would be good to have company, even a dog, especially now that it was growing dark.

Philip moved on, glancing back once to see what the dog was doing. It had stayed where he'd left it, still tending its burns. But an instant later it appeared at his side.

Philip nearly laughed with relief. "Okay," he said, gruffly. "You want to come? So, come on!"

He'd seen only four pools in the area between the Billings home and the hospital. He had counted them from the hill before dropping down to the housing development. All contained ash and debris. After finding a dead cat in the first pool, he peered anxiously in each of the others, fearful of finding worse.

Which pool would be best, one closest to the hospital or one with less debris? How should he know? How could he decide? He supposed Matt would choose quickly, and if Philip asked how he'd made the choice, Matt would probably say, "It's obvious." But it wasn't. It never was. To know what was right, or best, sometimes took so much weighing. Maybe just making a decision, any decision, was better than agonizing endlessly.

"Dog," he said at the third pool, after going back and forth several times. "It'll be this one. Now we've got to figure out how far it is to the hospital so I can get the right amount of hose. Where will I get that? And we're going to need a pump and some gas, Mr. Billings said. And a flashlight, because pretty soon I won't be able to see anything!"

The dog wagged his tail in sympathy and lapped at the cruddy water. Suddenly he turned and growled menacingly. Philip jumped. Approaching them was a man with a gun aimed at him. The man stopped about ten feet away. "Okay, hands up! Who are you? What are you doing? What do you want?"

Philip's mouth went dry and his heart began to pound. He lifted his hands slowly. He had thought the home to which the pool belonged was deserted because there had been no sign of life when he'd passed on the way to the backyard. The man's eyes looked strange, even from a distance, as if he couldn't see well. Could they have been affected by the bomb's light?

"I — I'm just checking to see if this water's drinkable. . . ."

"Yeah, sure! Hands up! Don't come any closer!"

He can't see well, Philip thought. His eyes must have been hurt by the flash. Slowly he bent to hold the dog's collar, shushing him, one hand still raised. "The hospital needs water! There's a DWP engineer on Via Carlotta who says we can pump it from pools to the hospital."

The man drew closer and peered at Philip.

"I don't believe you. You're just a kid. They're not gonna send a kid to do a man's job." He thrust the gun out aggressively and glanced around.

Philip began to sweat. He followed the man's gaze. Was he looking to see if Philip might have brought help, or *if someone might see him* when he pulled the trigger?

"Look, mister!" he cried. "Sssh, dog! Down! I'm not looking for trouble. I'm telling you, they're just going crazy at the hospital. Water pipes are broken and the bottled water's used up. There'll be help, but maybe not till tomorrow or the day after. Meanwhile, they need drinking water."

"I'm listening. . . ." The man kept the gun trained on him.

"So maybe your pool is polluted, but they'll know how to purify it. They can find out through Goleta; they've got radio contact there." Philip's heart was thumping so hard, he thought the man could hear it. "Mr. Billings said we need a pump. You got one? He says most pool owners in these hills have pumps so they can use their pool water in case of hill fires."

"Who's Billings?"

"The water and power guy I told you about!"

The man lowered his gun slowly. "Okay. Suppose I believe you. How you gonna get the water all the way to the hospital?"

Philip gestured downhill toward the hospital buildings. "I can't. Not alone. We'll

116

have to get to a hardware store, I suppose, and get what we need. Will you help me?"

Shakily the man wiped a hand across his eyes. "I can't leave. My wife's inside. She's pregnant."

What would radiation do to an unborn child? Philip shook the thought from his head. "She can stay at the Billings'. They're nearby." He paused. "By the way, my name's Philip." He waited a long, anxious minute before the man finally replied. "Grear. Jason Grear. And yes, I do have a pump, but it's not working."

Mr. Grear tucked the gun into his belt and walked slowly to the edge of his property where he could look down at the hospital below. "It's almost dark. We'll have to move fast. Eight hundred — a thousand feet of hose? Maybe. Don't know how we'll carry all that." He squinted through the gloom. "God, what chaos. And we're *lucky*. We weren't in L.A. And there's help coming. What would it be like if it was all-out war?" He shook his head and stepped back.

It was dark by the time they brought Mrs. Grear to the Billings' home and were on their way again, this time with a lantern. Despite his back pain, John Billings hobbled along on his crutches to the pool. There he remained to work on the pump while Philip and Jason Grear went after hoses. Philip had reluctantly tied up the dog, but its outraged bark followed him for a long time.

"How come you didn't take off like most of the others?" Philip asked as they made their way by back streets to the shopping plaza. Several times he'd reached a hand out to guide Grear, certain he didn't see obstacles until he was nearly on them.

"It's safer here, is why, even with the crazies running around. Can you imagine what it's gonna be like when the million or so scared people get to the desert? They'll be sick, out of food and water, desperate . . . and not enough camps set up to help them. Think the Palmdale and Lancaster residents are gonna open their homes to them? Unh-unh. Fifty refugees, maybe, a hundred. But a million?"

"But aren't you afraid to stay because of the fallout?"

"Aren't you?"

For a moment Philip considered the question. He hadn't had time to look ahead. Then he said, "Until my mom's on her way to a burn center and I've found my dad, I don't care what happens to me."

Grear cleared his throat and didn't speak for some moments, then he said, "The way I figure is that until they tell us where that cloud's gonna spill its poison, this place is good as any. With Wanda pregnant, we couldn't go far, anyway. We'll just wait and hope that army gets here soon and takes us all out to wherever it's safe."

And then what? Philip thought. Would

they ever be able to come back? Their home was gone. Without water or power and with all the devastation, they couldn't live here again for a long time.

As they came closer to the shopping center, Philip could see and *feel* the throbbing mass of refugees still moving along Verdugo Road across Foothill Boulevard, up Angeles Crest Highway to the mountains. He glimpsed the church spire and, for a hopeful moment, considered cutting through that thick rope of people to see if Cara and Matt were there. But he knew he mustn't. By now the hospital would be desperate for water. Other aides would be "liberating" the contents of hot-water tanks in nearby homes and appropriating distilled water from the nearest super-markets, if those machines still operated. But such measures hardly amounted to anything. It was like throwing a bucket of water on a huge fire. Even the nurse who had sent him to the DWP engineer seemed to doubt anything could really be done. Well, maybe she was right.

"Oh, God!" Philip exclaimed when they arrived at the shopping plaza. "Oh, no!"

That morning, when he'd first left the Giaimos with Cara, he'd seen death on the Crest Highway. He'd seen overturned cars and cars that had exploded, their victims entrapped behind wheels or incinerated. But he had seen it without letting it sink in. He had deliberately stayed his distance, partly because of Cara and partly because he had always been repulsed by death, ever since he'd been expected to kiss his grandfather goodbye when he died.

Now, in the shopping plaza, he saw death everywhere. A woman lay half-in and half-out of her car trunk. Two women, probably on their way into the Safeway at the moment of the burst, lay on the ground some distance away like broken dolls with empty eyes. A small breeze blew cartons and paper around the mangled steel.

And yet, people moved amidst this death. As they cut through the parking lot they surprised a man pushing a dead body aside to reach canned goods strewn inside the car. Two women were fighting, tearing at each other's faces and hair over a can of tomato juice. A woman with a child in her arms came out of the store sobbing, empty-handed. What food the store once displayed on its shelves had already been taken by the thousands of people on their way to the desert.

The glass window of Builder's Emporium had also blown in, and glass lay everywhere. Mr. Grear, leading the way, grunted as he nearly tripped, and at his feet Philip saw a man, mostly covered by debris. A shard of glass was embedded in his neck. He suppressed the nausea rising to his throat and moved on.

In the dim light he saw nothing but chaos. Heavy shelves were toppled. Tools, paint, kitchen utensils, and patio furniture — everywhere. Several men, startled by their presence, glanced up, then returned to their looting.

He could understand needing wagons or barrows, things with wheels that might carry loads, but these men were looting anything and everything, regardless of immediate usefulness.

"Over here," Grear said. "Under all this stuff."

Philip set down the lantern and began lifting the pipes and fittings, under which were the hoses. He had been working only a few moments when he sensed someone behind him, and suddenly the lantern disappeared.

"Hey!" he called, straightening up.

He turned to see a man holding a wrench in one hand and the lantern in the other.

"What are you doing? What you need garden hoses for? You gonna water your lawn?" The man laughed as if he'd just said something very funny.

"I'll take that lantern, buddy," Mr. Grear said. "You just go on about your own business and leave us to ours."

"Hey, guys!" the man called over his shoulder. "We need garden hoses, right?"

"No!" Philip cried, clutching one of the hoses to his chest. "We're trying to hook up water for the hospital."

"Hey, guys!" the man called again. "Some

good samaritans here. They got water somewhere. *Where,* kid? *Where?*" He held the
wrench threateningly.

"I'll take that lantern," Jason Grear said.
He was suddenly in front of Philip, and his
gun was drawn. "Get going or I'll use this."

"Oh, now, man!" The voice lost its cocki-
ness. "Okay, okay, we're just fooling around."

"Put it down. I'll count to three."

Philip moved closer to Mr. Grear, aware
that the other men in the store had come up
from behind.

"One ... two. ..."

The man looked around anxiously, expect-
ing help from his friends. When no one reacted, he slowly put the lantern down.

"The wrench, too."

"Yeah, sure, man." The wrench dropped
to the ground with a clatter.

Philip sensed a slight movement behind
him and turned quickly. One of the other men
seemed about to throw something. Without
thinking, Philip put himself between the man
and Grear. "I wouldn't do that!" he cried.

Grear swung around abruptly and fired.
The shot made a loud ping on metal nearby.
"I'm not much on killing," he said. "There
are enough dead already from this 'accident,'
but if I have to. ..."

No one moved. Philip's legs trembled. He
could smell the sweat of fear all around him.
Did Grear deliberately miss, or hadn't he
been able to see well enough?

"Okay, you creeps," Grear said after a

moment. "This is how it's gonna be. You're gonna be real men for a change. You're gonna be patriots! Now get your butts over here and pick up these hoses, then come along with us." He waved the gun around to emphasize his words.

As the men moved forward and began searching under the rubble, Grear put a hand on Philip's arm. "Don't disappoint me," he whispered, pressing the gun into his hand. Softly he added, "I can hardly see."

Philip's sweaty hand closed on the hard metal. He had once held a BB gun and shot it at squirrels and birds with a ten-year-old friend. But when the friend had hit a bird, he'd vowed never to touch a gun again. He licked dry lips and stepped back, beyond reach. Breathing hard, hand unsteady, he raised the gun and held it on the men.

What if they ran off? What if they turned on him? Could he pull the trigger?

Chapter 12

The five of them left the shopping center together. Four men carried heavy lengths of hose and one — Philip — brandished a gun he was not sure he could use.

A breeze had started up, not the dry, dusty Santa Ana type wind of the desert, but a stirring of moisture-laden air from the sea. Mixed with it was the harsh smell of burning and something new, a sickeningly sweet smell. It was especially strong when they passed a body.

If the winds had turned, Philip immediately thought, then the atomic cloud would be drifting back over Los Angeles. Was it already dropping its poisonous particles? Was that why he felt so tired now, as if he had gone without rest for days? Was that why he ached everywhere, why his legs trembled and a nagging hunger-nausea plagued his stomach? Would all this effort be pointless in the end because water would only keep alive those who would soon die of radiation?

He dragged along behind the men, trying to appear alert, fighting an almost over-whelming desire to collapse and cry and then sleep.

The men carrying the hoses noted the wind shift, too. They glanced back at Philip frequently, as if hoping to catch him off-guard. About a block from the plaza one of them dropped his load and would have slid off into the darkness if Philip hadn't instantly rushed to his side, gun leveled.

The others stopped, too, waiting.

"Pick those up," Philip ordered. His voice was high but he kept direct eye contact with the man.

"Like hell! Kill me if you want, what difference does it make? Look." He started to walk off. Immediately the others dropped their loads and followed.

"Shoot!" Jason Grear cried. "*Philip, shoot!*"

Philip shakily raised the gun, then shook his head and lowered it. He couldn't. He wasn't a killer. He heard the men crashing over obstacles in their rush to get away in the dark, and he didn't care. "Here," he said, holding the gun by its barrel and handing it back to Grear. "I'm sorry."

"*Now* how do we get all these hoses up the hill? Damn you, kid! You could have fired over their heads!"

Philip began stacking hoses, trying to figure how he could carry ten at once. "I'll carry half," he said.

Grear laughed bitterly. "You?"

"You got a better idea?" Philip cried, hurt by the inference.

"I'm sorry, kid. Try it." Grear bent to pick up one of the dropped hoses. "We'll get them up to Billings one way or another."

The trail of evacuees had not lessened, though it was now dark. Philip trudged along, carrying half his weight in hoses, thinking of happy times. It was a trick he'd often used when he ran, to keep himself from feeling pain.

Cara's bright face came to mind. He pictured the way her almond-shaped eyes opened in amusement when he said something funny. He thought for the hundredth time of the day he'd almost kissed her. He'd walked her home from school and told her about the song he was writing. Her eyes had turned gentle, and he wanted then to hold her close, to feel what it was like having a girl's body against his, and then to kiss her. But as he was speaking, heat rising to his face as these thoughts intruded, he worried. How should he do it? Should he just put his arm around her waist, then turn her toward him? What if she pulled back, was repulsed by his boldness? What if his breath was bad or his nose got in his way? So many things could go wrong. And then the moment was lost.

If he had kissed her then, he'd often thought, would she still have become Matt's girl friend?

The dog announced their approach with

hysterical barks. Back to reality, he again felt the ache in his shoulders, the cramp in his left leg, and the burning in his chest. By force of will he propelled himself the last few yards and dumped the hoses in a heap near Mr. Billings. Then he dropped to his haunches and took deep, gulping breaths. He angrily wiped away the tears that slid down his cheeks.

"Any problems?" John Billings asked of Mr. Grear, who was straightening up with obvious pain.

"None whatever."

"Good. I've got the pump going. Found some gas that didn't blow up, stuff we kept for the mower. Don't know how long it will work, but let's give it a go."

Philip rose, blinked his eyes, and came forward, picking up two hoses as he moved. Grear began stripping the cardboard wrappers from the hoses, and Mr. Billings was busily attaching the first two hoses to the pump.

In the stillness Philip heard more helicopter activity nearby. A long beam of light pierced the darkness, focusing on the only building with power, the hospital. It had been several hours since he'd left his mother. He worried that she might be neglected in the crush of other victims. He agonized that he'd made the wrong decision to leave her, even with the nurse's promises.

"They've started landing," Billings said, as if he could read Philip's mind. He nodded in the direction of the helicopter pad at the hospital. "Maybe they'll be airlifting the burn victims out. Now let's get this hose in the water, deep enough so it'll bypass the crud, then we'll turn it on and hope."

A few moments later the three of them stood grinning at each other as the first drops of water trickled, then flowed from the hose onto the ground. The water appeared to be clear. Most of the ash and other debris had settled to the pool bottom or remained floating at the top.

For the next few minutes they ripped off the new hose wrappings and connected the first long lengths together as the dog barked for attention nearby. Philip took a moment to release the dog, who jumped up on him, wildly wagging his tattered tail and giving slobbery kisses. Philip laughingly shooed him off as he worked with Mr. Grear. Together they unwound coils of hose and connected them end to end, making their way down the slope and across a no-man's land of burned homes. With each fifty-foot length they drew closer to the hospital.

The hospital parking lot was lit by fires and lanterns, and as crowded with wounded as when he'd left. The sound of helicopters moving in the darkness gave him hope that his mother might already be gone. Voices, hammering, and other sounds of life filtered up the hill to where they worked.

"You run ahead and see where they want this water delivered," Grear said as he coupled one of the last hoses. "I'll finish here — can't see too well, anyway. I'll keep the mutt." Philip started to uncoil the long hose and work it downhill.

"Go on, Philip. You did a good job. Your folks ought to be very proud. When our boy's born, I just hope he becomes half the man *you* are."

Philip flushed in the darkness and took the lantern. It was to be used as a signal to Mr. Billings to start the pump. As he moved off in the darkness, jumping and sliding down the rocky slope, he found himself savoring Grear's words. *Man*, he'd been called. He couldn't remember anyone ever making him feel so good.

Philip tapped the arm of the first person who appeared to be in authority at the parking lot. A doctor, he assumed by the man's bloodstained white coat.

"Excuse me, sir. I've brought pool water down from up there." He motioned to the dark housing project in the hills nearby. "We've hooked up hoses and as soon as we know where to deliver it, we'll turn on the pump."

The doctor glanced at him, then returned to the patient he was tending. He pocketed a stethoscope and reached for the patient's wrist. "Go away."

Go away? Why, he thinks I'm making this up, thinks I'm crazy, Philip thought in dismay. Just because I don't have muscles or whiskers and a deep voice that makes people listen, he doesn't believe me!

Philip tugged at the doctor's arm again, angry now. "Doctor! You've got to listen to me. I'm not kidding!"

"Listen, boy, you want to be useful, go inside and bring out some more D5W if they have any!"

"But, the water!" Philip looked behind him at the small light moving on the slope where Mr. Grear was descending. "Look, up there!" He pulled harder on the doctor.

"Nurse!"

A nurse nearby scurried over.

"Get this kid off of me. I've got enough trouble without him pestering me!"

"Philip!" the nurse cried, recognizing him. "What's going on?"

"You know this boy?"

"Yes! He was a great help here most of the day. We sent him to find a DWP engineer." She turned to Philip. "You look so tired! What happened?"

Philip explained about finding Mr. Billings and about how they had arranged to pump water down to the hospital. "We can keep moving the pump to other pools, except some of the water is probably pretty contaminated."

"You did it, you really did!" the nurse cried. "Well, let's not just stand here. We need that water! I'll get the maintenance people to help. We've got a storage tank on the roof. And don't worry about contamination. We know how to handle that!"

"How's my mom?" Philip asked, trailing after the nurse.

But the nurse only answered, "Oh, my, what a relief to have water coming at last!" and began giving orders.

Twenty minutes later he stood beside Mr. Grear in the crowded hospital lot looking up at the dark, invisible hill where Mr. Billings would be waiting. The final hose had been connected to a roof tank. A maintenance man had called down that they were ready to receive.

Philip swung the lantern back and forth three times, paused, then swung it again. Somewhere in that darkness Mr. Billings was watching. He would go to the pump and start the flow. If all went well the water would soon be sucked up through the hose in the pool and begin running through the long stretch of hoses to the hospital. For what seemed a terribly long time Philip stared into the darkness, and then to the rooftop, waiting for word. Finally an excited cry rang out. "It's coming!"

"Mom . . ." he whispered, leaning over his mother. "Mom. . . ."

His mother didn't answer. He felt her cold skin and weak pulse, and a wave of fear swept through him. He grabbed at the nurse who had assured him of her care. "Why hasn't she been airlifted? You've had helicopters landing for the last hour! Why hasn't my mother been taken out?"

The nurse cried out and dropped the pitcher she was holding. The plastic clattered noisily to the floor, and its dark contents spilled out in all directions. She started to scream, and stuffed a fist against her lips. Then a loud, piercing wail came from her throat.

Philip grabbed her arms. "Stop that! Stop it! What about my mother? She looks terrible! Will she be all right?"

One of the maintenance men rushed up and pulled the nurse away. "Leave her alone. Can't you see she's exhausted? She's been on duty more than twenty-four hours! She doesn't know what she's doing anymore."

"My mother! She promised. . . ." He closed his mouth. It was useless to blame anyone. The emergency rooms smelled of blood and vomit and even death; they were even more crowded than when he'd left. Even with more people helping — maybe people flown in — there weren't enough.

He went back to his mother. He shouldn't have left her. Where was Matt? Why wasn't *he* here? What could he do?

He tried offering water, but the drops slid down her swollen lips to her neck. He rushed from room to room searching for something, for someone to help. But it was like an old movie where the film is speeded up and the sound comes out garbled.

He stopped suddenly and pressed a hand to his forehead to block out everything except his thoughts. It was stupid running around so pointlessly. He had to have a plan. He had to do something positive or his mother would die!

He ran out to the parking lot, to the doctor he had first approached. "Doctor! Please! Will you look at my mother and tell me what to do? Please, come inside!"

The doctor shook him off. "Can't you see I've got my hands full out here? Get someone inside to check her!"

"There's no one, no one! Please! You owe me!" He started to cry, sobbing shamelessly, like a small, frightened child. He wiped his eyes with the back of his hand, ashamed to be bartering for his mother's life.

"All right, son, all right. Where is she?" The doctor ran beside Philip into the building, ignoring pleas for help from those he passed.

Philip watched, fist jammed against his mouth, as the doctor bent over his mother. At last he straightened up and turned thoughtfully to Philip. "It's not good. I'll order another IV, but she should be at a burn center."

He could hardly get the words out. "Will she make it?"

"I don't know. I'm sorry. I really don't know."

Philip lowered his head, not wanting to cry again. Then he crouched beside his mother, searching for a flicker of an eye, some movement that would indicate life. "Mom . . ." he whispered. "Don't die! I love you. . . . We need you." He swallowed hard and stood up.

He didn't care how many people were lined up to be flown out. One way or another he'd get his mother on the next helicopter headed for a burn center.

Chapter 13

"Two or three at a time? That's all?" Philip cried, his voice rising in disbelief.

He had watched from behind the dispatcher as three patients were transferred to litters, logged out, and loaded onto the noisy helicopter in the center of the helipad. The chopper door had been slammed shut, and the machine lifted from the ground in a wild *whoosh* of hurricanelike wind and noise. For an instant it hovered as if uncertain of its purpose, then it swerved off into the darkness.

The man guarding the exit door from the hospital to the helipad turned to answer Philip. His eyes were slitted against the dust, and a hand covered his nose. "Who are you? You're not supposed to be here!"

"Those 'copters can only take out two or three people at a time?" Philip replied, stubbornly ignoring the dismissal.

"Right! They're from Pacoima. Fire Department. The whole county's only got five of them! We've been promised Coast Guard choppers, but I haven't seen any yet, and the Army and Marines should be sending in. . . . Listen, kid. You're not supposed to be here!"

"My mother's inside, badly burned," he said, motioning toward the emergency room some distance away. "She's supposed to be flown out to a burn center."

"Yeah, her and a thousand others." The man nodded to a large room off to the side. It was filled with wounded on stretchers and gurneys. "Sorry, kid. She'll have to wait."

"She can't!" Philip cried, dogging the man's heels. He knew he shouldn't be so pushy, but he couldn't seem to stop himself. "Mister, wait!"

"You can't come in here," a nurse said, turning him away from the holding room with a firm hand on his arm. In the brief instant before the door closed, he saw several attendants in green hospital garb. On the nearest gurney he noticed a number, pinned to the sheet covering.

For a long moment he waited at the closed door, wanting to force his way in, knowing it would get him nowhere. With only three people being airlifted out every ten minutes or so, it could take hours before the wounded in just that one room would be moved. In the meantime his mother could die. His whole body shook as he turned on his heels and ran back to the emergency room.

He was passing the radio room when a voice saying "burn centers" stopped him. The voice faded, then returned, stronger. "Sorry,

Glendale. We're trying to get to you. Clear a landing space — a hundred by a hundred — and set up some signal fires so we can see."

"We did that already! At the high school playground. Can't you see our fires? For God's sake, man. Where's the help you promised?"

Someone in the radio room switched stations and started speaking. Philip looked into the room and saw a white-coated man at the radio.

"This is Verdugo Hospital, calling Goleta. Verdugo Hospital to Goleta."

"Goleta Police. Captain Arquette speaking."

"This is Dr. Cuba. We've got a thousand wounded here, at least half of them burns. Where're the medics to take them out? We've got choppers taking two, three at a time. What is this, a joke?"

"Sorry, doctor. We've got requests to take out victims from everywhere. Military choppers are on the way."

"It's been thirty hours! These burns need attention!"

There was just the slightest hesitation, and then Goleta returned with, "The whole of California's got fewer than two hundred beds for severe burn victims, doctor. You must know that! The beds are full. Personnel are supervising other medical staff so they can serve maybe five, six hundred. That's it. We're sending to Arizona now."

"Arizona? Christ!"

Philip's breath caught in his throat. If California could only treat two hundred severely burned, what could the less populated Arizona possibly have — ten, twenty-five, even fifty beds? As he hurried back to his mother he remembered a conversation he'd heard and paid no attention to weeks ago. "Listen to this," his father had said in an incredulous tone. "Some government official says we could survive all-out nuclear war with maybe thirty to forty percent of our population intact." *How*, Philip now wondered bitterly, *with hospitals gone, doctors dead or dying, medical supplies destroyed, water contaminated, fires everywhere, and even the air we breathe poisoned?* And what of those few who did survive? What could they live on? What about the diseases and illness that would follow? He was sure, as he thought about it, that he'd rather die quickly than be one of the unlucky ones who lived.

A sickening anguish filled his stomach. Until yesterday he'd tuned out everything except what happened in his own small world of school, music, running, his family and friends. Now he realized he'd been stupid, that he should have paid attention to what was happening elsewhere. If grown-ups were so dumb as to keep building bombs and threatening each other like kids with snowballs, then maybe grown-ups weren't any smarter than kids.

He didn't know if his mother heard him as

he bent over her still, clammy-cool body, but he spoke anyway, whispering in her ear.

"Mom, listen. Hang in there, please. I'm going to get you out of here. Just hold on another hour or two, and you'll be where they know just what to do for your burns."

He thought his mother's hand tightened slightly in his, but he wasn't sure.

First he had to move his mother's gurney out of the crowded room. Harried, he looked around. The attendant who was caring for the fifty or so patients had left for more supplies. The patients were jammed so tightly together that there was practically no space between them. Some, against the walls, might not have been examined in hours because they were so inaccessible. His mother's bed stood in the middle of the room. To move her out he'd have to rearrange other patients. It reminded him of those puzzles he used to love working, where you had to line up numbers in consecutive order with only one free space to move in. If he pushed that bed to there, and that one to —

"Phil!"

He swung around, joy surging through his limbs at the sound of his brother's voice.

"Matt! Cara!"

Dark rings rimmed Cara's eyes, and Matt wore a two-day stubble of beard. They looked ragged and disheveled and tired beyond caring. He realized that he must look the same.

The sound of a helicopter coming in cut

short his pleasure. Though he wanted to know where they had been, what had happened since he'd left them, and why they hadn't come sooner, he thought now only of his mother.

"Move that bed to the right, Matt, will you, and Cara, move that one to the left."

"Hey, wait! How's Mom?"

"Matt, please!" The chopper sounded closer now. It would be landing in another moment. If he could get their mother out quickly, then maybe. . . . "Move that bed Matt!"

"Why? What are you doing?"

"Just do it!" He began sliding another gurney aside, so that soon there'd be space to move his mother out. As he worked he explained about the helicopters taking out the burn victims and how the burn centers in California were already overcrowded. If they didn't get their mother out soon, there'd be no hospital with specialized care in the whole country that wasn't filled.

"Just what are you kids doing?" a voice cried, outraged.

"Don't stop, Matt! Do what I said!" Philip ordered as Matt paused to look uncertainly from him to the attendant.

"You leave those beds alone! Go on! Get out of here before I call security."

Security. Some joke, Philip thought. "We'll put everyone back exactly as they were. We're just rolling our mother out so we can take care of her ourselves." He figured it was wiser not to speak of his plans in case someone tried to stop him.

"You can't *do* anything for her! We've triaged the patients."

"Triaged?" Cara asked in a weak voice.

"Sorted out, set priorities on. Those we can help, those who could survive if we got them to a burn center are identified with tags." The attendant's patience seemed about gone. "Look, you kids get out of here. I'm sorry about your mother, but these patients won't make it."

"Then you won't mind if we take our mother where we can be with her for a while," Philip said grimly, pushing another bed out of the way. "Matt. . . ." He started to slide his mother's gurney into the space that opened up. "Put the other patients back where they were, like we said."

The fact that they were returning the other beds to their original positions as he'd said they would seemed to placate the attendant. He muttered irritably about not having enough help or supplies and left the room.

"What the heck are you up to?" Matt whispered. He and Cara caught up to Philip and fell in beside him while he pushed his mother through the halls towards the stairs leading to the lower level and the heliport. "Mom. . . ." Matt touched his mother's hand, felt for a pulse. His face flushed. "Mom!"

"Matt, there's a storeroom down that hall. It's got lots of those green scrub gowns. I need one. Get it please!"

"My God! Look at her! She's dying!" Matt pulled at Philip's arm. "Why weren't you seeing she got proper care!"

"Matt . . ." Cara cried, pulling at his arm.

Philip wanted to scream, *Where were you, brother, all this time?* He wanted to scream, *Shut up, smart ass! She's not going to die. She's not! I won't let her!* Instead he said, "Get that gown, like I said, and some rubber gloves if you see them. Hurry! The helicopter will be leaving any second!"

"Where?" Cara asked. "Come on, Matt. Help me find what he wants!"

For a second Matt still gripped Philip's arm, screaming accusations, then his hand dropped away. He turned and hurried off, with Cara, to the storeroom.

For the first time in his life Philip didn't feel that old sense of inadequacy, that terrible call-to-arms feeling he always got when his brother put him down, the feeling that set him screaming irrationally in self-defense. He'd done the best he could; he didn't know what else he might have done under the circumstances.

As they entered the final corridor before reaching the holding room where the patients were moved out to the choppers, Philip stopped. "You guys better stay here. They'll be suspicious if they see the three of us. I'll put on the scrub gown and hope they don't recognize me. I've changed the tag Mom's wearing so she doesn't look hopeless."

"Maybe I should take her in," Matt said. "They haven't seen me around."

Philip considered that for an instant, warring with himself over giving this last step to his brother. It was true that he might be recognized. Matt would not be, and he appeared older, more authoritative. But he wouldn't let Matt take over, and it wasn't for ego reasons. It was something he had to do himself because he could do it better than Matt. He had a trait Matt didn't have, a trait the family usually disliked him for because it was so uncompromising. Stubbornness. Persistence beyond reason. When he wanted something, he went after it and worked for it or fought for it and hung on and pushed and sought loopholes and other exits until he got what he wanted most of the time. Matt wasn't like that. If *he* took their mother into that room and tried to get her on a chopper he might be stopped. He might not find another way or push hard enough. The one thing Philip knew about himself, whether it was a good trait or not, was that he'd get his mother on a chopper somehow. Nothing and no one would stop him.

He could hear voices, wheels rolling along the corridor to the outside, and the whir of helicopter blades at idle. "I think *I'd* better do it, Matt. Be back as soon as I can." Without waiting for Matt's response he donned the scrub gown, pushed the cap over his dark hair, and wiped his face to get off some of the soot and char. And then he turned the corner into the corridor leading to the outside heli-pad. An attendant in a green scrub gown just like his was rolling a gurney out the door. The guard with a clipboard checked the patient through.

"Hold up!" he called, trying to deepen the timbre of his voice while controlling its tremble. He started down the corridor at a run, pushing his mother on the gurney. "This one goes priority. Wait up!"

Chapter 14

"Wait a *minute*! Priority? Who says?" The guard at the exit door blocked him with his body. "Where's her tag?"

"Tag? Tag? You kidding?" Ahead he saw the chopper, its blades whirling slowly. A litter was being lifted into its cabin. Heart pounding, eyes moving from chopper to guard to chopper, he cried, "It's a madhouse back there! Who's got time to tag anyone?" He swallowed, forcing himself to look the guard squarely in the eyes. "She's to go out immediately, Dr. Watkins' orders!" Albe Watkins had been the doctor who'd yanked his disjointed finger back in place in the hospital just last year.

"Watkins, huh? Yeah, well. . . ." The physician's name gave credibility. "Okay, but move her to the holding room. Priority or not, we got sixty patients ahead of her. Nurse'll give you a number."

Philip hesitated, wanting to press further; the helicopter was only yards away, and its rotors were picking up speed. The attendant who had carried out the last patient was returning with an empty litter, his body bent forward against the roaring wind as the chopper lifted.

Too late. He'd have to wait for the next airlift, or the next. Disappointed and frustrated, he rolled the gurney to the holding room.

He was given a number by a nurse who regarded his mother doubtfully. "This one's been triaged to fly out? She looks —"

Philip cut her short. "Dr. Watkins says she's borderline, that's why the priority."

"They're all priority!" The nurse wrote number fifty-seven on a card and gave it to him. He almost protested, realizing fifty-six others would be flown out before they'd take his mother, but he stopped himself. "Put her there," she said, pointing. "Then you can go on back." Her suspicious glance made him uneasy, and he hurriedly rolled his mother away.

Around them lay people who were crying or moaning or tossing about restlessly in pain. Why didn't his mother move or cry out? At least it would show she was alive! He pushed her to the place the nurse had indicated, then bent over the IV control, pretending to make adjustments while his mind raced, trying to figure out how to stay there. As a runner he'd be expected to return to emergency for the next patient, but he had no intention of leaving.

The heavy flap of another 'copter diverted the nurse's attention. "We got a big one coming in!" the dispatcher yelled, sticking his head in the door. "Marine CH-53, hanging a water buffalo." A moment later he was back. "Should take a dozen, maybe fifteen, soon as it's unloaded!"

"Okay, let's move 'em," the nurse cried. "Let's go!" Philip fell in behind the other orderlies and started moving gurneys into the hallway. Through the open door he saw a big tank suspended from a heavy chain, swinging on its platform as it lowered to the ground. *A water buffalo?*

The attendant in front of him said, "Yeah, I've seen those things. They usually pull them behind six-wheel trucks. They hold maybe fifteen hundred gallons of water."

A bright search beam fixed on the landing pad, then seconds later the helicopter set down. Almost immediately the door slid open and about thirty men dropped down. They came running into the building carrying boxes Philip supposed contained medical supplies and food. The Marines dispersed to the supply rooms, along with an orderly who was instructed to bring back anyone who could hook up the water tank. A tall, young Marine doctor began examining the patients in the hallway, with the nurse at his side.

Philip's heart beat faster, and his face became warm. Maybe, he thought, in the confusion he could slip his mother in among those in the hall. It was worth a try. He returned to the holding room and went to her.

Her eyes were wide open, but they were dark and expressionless as she stared at the ceiling. "Mom!" he cried, a wave of relief spreading through him. Her hands clutched the sheet, tight-fisted, as if the pain was hardly bearable. Only the eyes moved. She was seeing him but not responding. It was as if she had escaped inward and all her energies were focused on control.

He was so close to exhaustion that the sight of his mother's pain nearly broke him. Instead he sucked in his breath, turned his eyes away, and carefully pushed the gurney from the room so as not to cause additional pain.

Out in the hallway the commotion of Marines passing back and forth with boxes and of gurneys moving toward the exit door and out to the helipad helped mask his deception. He moved to the end of the line, eyes so intent on the nurse and doctor, three patients away, that he feared they would sense it. He tried to appear unconcerned, as if the patient beside him meant no more than any other, but his heart pounded in his ears, and his neck itched with sweat. Any moment now they would move on to the next patient, and then the next, and then they would stop at his mother.

He moved forward. The loaded gurneys were rolling swiftly through the exit door to the helicopter, and just as swiftly returning empty for new patients. His whole body trembled as the doctor approached their gurney.

The paper pinned to his mother's bed sheet showed the percent of second- and third-degree burns. Glancing first at the paper, then taking his mother's hand for a pulse, the doctor said, "She's in great pain. Demerol."

"Wait a minute!" the nurse cried, noticing Philip for the first time and checking the number. "She's out of turn! The next patient should be twenty-four."

"Please!" Philip cried. "Please take her!"

"There's only room for twelve. Orderly? Bring out the next patient."

"Is this your mother, son?" the doctor asked.

"Yes!"

The doctor barely hesitated. "Nurse, don't hold us up. Give her the shot. Let's keep things moving. Go on, son. Take her out."

He was so grateful that he wanted to laugh and cry at the same time. Before the doctor could change his mind, he covered his mother's face as he'd seen the other orderlies do before they pushed their patients out to the helipad — then ran. He ran past the guard at the door, across the dusty, windy stretch of no-man's land to the waiting chopper. There, helping hands raised her aboard before he could say good-bye or good luck or I love you or anything. And he suddenly found himself back at the exit door with great big knobs of pain in his throat as the big bird rose skyward with its load of burn victims — and his mom.

He let out his breath. He felt as if he'd been holding it for hours. The chopper swooped up, then swung off into the darkness, its small lights flickering.

Thank you, God, he whispered silently. *Thank you. Take good care of her. Keep her alive, and I'll never doubt again.* He pushed the gurney back down the hall, light-headed and as empty as the gurney, and sad now, in a way that he'd never felt before. Would someone else's mom or dad die because his mother had taken their place on the chopper? He didn't want to think about that. It seemed to him it was the only thing he could have done, but he didn't like having done it. He owed a heavy debt, and he could think of no way to repay it except to keep going.

Cara and Matt were not where he'd left them, so he went on to the emergency room. "Take a rest, kid," a Marine said, removing the gurney from him. "We'll take it from here." The rooms were peppered with uniformed Marines, so he moved out to the parking lot.

It was a different scene from before. Lights had been set up to illuminate the large space, and most of the cars had been removed to make space for more patients. In the distance he heard the rumble of heavy equipment. He heard trucks and bulldozers and the almost constant *flap-flap* of helicopter movement.

It was late, well after midnight, and the human traffic to the mountains had slowed. He blinked burning eyes as he looked around for his brother and Cara. He let himself imagine being in his own bed again, feeling the smooth, cool surface of the sheets as he slid a foot downward, smelling the familiar scent of his own pillow as he buried his nose in it. He wrapped his arms around his chest, cold from fatigue and the night air. And then he saw Cara.

She was making out name tags at a table with several others. As soon as she saw him her tired eyes brightened, and she jumped up. They ran to each other like magnets about to collide. And then they were hugging and laughing with relief and delight to be together and still alive. Philip couldn't recall ever feeling a greater happiness.

"Hey, mister! That's *my* girl!" It was Matt's voice, and his hand was on Philip's shoulder. Philip swung around to find his brother grinning at him. A two-day growth of beard gave his face a dirty look, but his eyes were bright with happiness.

"Hey, ugly!" he returned. "You're gonna have to fight for her!" Laughing, they wrapped arms around each other, hugging with viselike grips.

After an awkward moment they pulled apart and Matt asked, "How's Mom? Did she get off okay?"

"She's on her way to Arizona, a burn center there."

"Any trouble?"

"Trouble? Heck, no. Easy as one of Horgan's workouts."

Matt regarded him seriously. "I bet. . . ."

For a moment they stared at each other with a mixture of affection and some of the same challenging competitiveness that was always there, close to the surface. Philip, four inches shorter, didn't feel the difference that had always bothered him before. Though he'd talked of fighting for Cara in jest, he realized with a twinge of surprise that he meant it. "So," he said, "where were you guys all day? Playing tiddlywinks?" He grinned. It was a tired imitation of his father's grin whenever he gave that explanation of his day's work.

"Did you hear that, Cara?" Matt responded in mock irritation. He moved close to Cara and put an arm lightly around her shoulder. "*He* was probably sleeping while we were slaving away at the church."

Cara shrugged Matt's arm away and took his hand instead. With her other hand she reached for Philip's. "What do we do now?"

Philip felt like the question was directed at him, but Matt answered. "Looks like things are under control here, so let's get some rest."

In the time they had been speaking, other helicopters had come in with more personnel and supplies. Some were fanning out to the main roads and were beginning to move disabled vehicles out of the way. Several times they had been told to move, and they'd even been asked once to leave the grounds.

"Let's go find Dad," Philip said.

"You're crazy! It's two A.M. I'm beat! We're all beat! I can't stand how grungy I feel!" Matt nodded at Cara. "Cara wants to get home and see if her mom's returned."

"Okay, we'll take her there, then go on."

"That's stupid! In a couple of hours the place will be swarming with outside help. If we got some sleep now we could just hitch a ride into Pasadena in the daylight instead of hiking all that distance in the dark.

"Nine, ten miles — that's all it is, Matt."

"It's dark, *stupid!* People are out there with guns, shooting anything that moves near them!"

"Don't call me stupid, Matt. I'm not!"

"Okay, okay. I'm sorry. You're not. But it's dumb to keep going when I can hardly think, I'm so trashed."

For a moment neither spoke, then Philip said, "They'll start evacuating as soon as those roads clear. We'll never find Dad then!"

"There'll be central information banks. He'll find us."

Again they stared at each other. For just a moment Philip doubted his judgment. Usually he bowed to Matt's wishes because his brother always seemed to be right, seemed to know what was best. But suddenly it seemed that Matt was just being stubborn. Inflexible. Here they were going through the same song-and-dance they always went through. And at the end *he'd* be the one expected to back down, not Matt. He'd be the one made to feel stupid or wrong.

Not this time.

"I want to see about Dad, Matt. I just want to. He may need help like Mom did. And I promised Mom." He paused. "You don't have to come."

"Don't worry! I won't! And not because I don't love Dad as much as you do. I just think it's pointless when we'll get help in only a few hours."

"Oh, come on, you two. You're acting like babies," Cara cried. "Why can't two brothers get along?"

"Last chance, Matt. Coming?" Philip asked stubbornly.

Matt hesitated. Philip knew his brother never expected that he'd hold out under pressure. "No."

"Okay." Although he spoke calmly, it hurt that Matt wouldn't come with him. His throat tightened at the prospect of going it alone, and he was so very tired. He couldn't look at Matt. Maybe he'd go back to the Billings and get the dog. Yeah, he'd feel safer with him along. Someone to talk to, to warn him if. . . .

"When I find Dad, I'll try to get back to the Giaimos' with him," he said. "S'long." He turned on his heels and headed out of the hospital parking lot.

He began to doubt the wisdom of his decision. Maybe he *should* wait until daylight.

Maybe Matt was right that they might get a ride into Pasadena. But maybe he wasn't. Who could predict what it would be like? Everyone needed help. Maybe people would be stopped from going in any direction except away from the city. Maybe everyone would be herded into trucks and taken out of the area.

He wanted to cry. He felt abandoned. But he wouldn't change his mind. Not this time.

He guessed Cara was right. If even brothers couldn't agree, how could countries? If there weren't so many nuclear bombs around, maybe that "accident" would never have happened. He guessed that if life ever returned to something like normal, he'd be a bit more tuned in to what was happening in the world. And maybe he'd even try to do something, somehow. He didn't know what, exactly — but something to stop grown-ups from playing "chicken" with bombs.

He had trudged halfway up the slope toward the Billings' place when he heard the dog's welcoming bark. He wiped the wetness from his cheeks with a hand and hurried on.

"Phil! Philip, wait!"

He stopped and looked back. In the bright lights of the hospital parking lot he saw Matt, climbing the hill toward him, pulling Cara along. "Hey, turkey, *wait*!"

"F— you," he said under his breath and kept climbing. And then it occurred to him that that was exactly what the Russians and Americans were always doing. Whenever one reached out a hand, the other backed off. He kicked at a rock in his path and stopped again as Matt called.

"Shake it, buddy!" he shouted back, "I haven't got all night!" He felt a rush of relief and joy spreading through him. Grinning, he started back down the slope to help them.